Partners
and
Strangers

Thanks for reading!

[signature]

Partners and Strangers

Michael Don

Carnegie Mellon University Press
Pittsburgh 2019

Acknowledgments

I am grateful to the editors and staff at the following journals where some of the stories in this book first appeared, occasionally under different titles:

Bluestem Magazine: "Yoav Feinberg's Last Year at Home"; *The Cortland Review*: "Will You Please Comply?"; *Fiction International*: "Control"; *Juked*: "Rules"; *Mayday Magazine*: "Problems We Can't Name"; *Per Contra*: "Zeros and Ones"; *The Southampton Review*: "A Home for an Eggplant"; *Sou'wester*: "A Normal Walk"; *Wag's Revue*: "In the Family"; *Washington Square Review*: "The Best Delivery Service"

My deepest thanks to all of my teachers, colleagues, friends, and family who have supported, advised, encouraged, inspired, and challenged me while working on this project.

Thanks especially to Jonathan Strong for the hundreds of pages read, and the years of mentorship and friendship, beginning at Tufts University. From the University of Illinois, I thank Audrey Petty and Alex Shakar for careful attention to and feedback on many of these stories, and for pushing me to keep revising. To Laura Adamczyk for always insightful feedback, and for reading recommendations and camaraderie. Thanks also to Max Somers, Sara Gelston, Eric Tanyavutti, Sean Karns, Aaron Burch, Amanda Bales, Michael Madonick, and Bruce Erickson who have been supportive colleagues, mentors, and friends.

Thanks to Baird Harper and Ted Weesner whose classes inspired me.

Thanks to the University of Illinois MFA program; to The Kikwetu Writers' Circle, especially John Obwavo; to the Colgate University Writers' Conference, especially Matt Leone, Carrie Brown, and Greg Ames; and to the Carnegie Mellon University Press editors and staff.

Thanks to Peter Balakian for support and guidance; and to Helen Kebabian, Jan Balakian, and Molly Schen for encouragement and reading recommendations.

Thanks to my parents, Carol and Irl Don, for your love and support, and bringing me into the world.

Most importantly, thanks to Sophia for your partnership: your wisdom, love, and encouragement know no bounds.

Book design by Connie Amoroso

Library of Congress Control Number 2018956031
ISBN 978-0-88748-650-0
Copyright © 2019 by Michael Don
Printed and bound in the United States of America

10 9 8 7 6 5 4 3 2 1

Contents

The Best Delivery Service

"You can call this number and order anything you want. Anything," Shira, my sister, tells me. I think I know what she's suggesting, but I doubt the science and technology exist, so instead, after she takes off for work, I call in a bucket of soft-shell crabs.

"Alive?" the man asks. The reception is so clear we could be talking face-to-face, though I suspect we're in different time zones.

"Sure," I say.

"Small, medium, or large?"

"Um, mix them up."

"That'll be twenty minutes. Any instructions for the delivery man?"

"Just leave them at the door," I say. "Oh, and if he has trouble finding my place, just tell him not to bother and to go back exactly the way he came."

The crabs show up in a red plastic bucket, no branding, no bar codes, a couple of small holes, and a receipt taped to the lid. They smell salty and fresh. If only it were summer and we lived within a few hundred miles of the ocean, then it'd make good sense. But it's not and we do not, so I decide there must be another rational way of thinking about this.

I look out over the row of terracotta rooftops and try to focus on the snowcapped peaks on the horizon to make certain I am where I am, but they are fuzzy and shapeless, so I get a funny feeling in my stomach. Up close, though, I know them to be hard and sturdy and permanent and I trust they will keep us in.

The bucket rocks gently, scooting an inch here, an inch there. I lift the lid and nudge it over with my foot, search the mail and then go back inside not waiting to see in which direction they scurry off.

"Any cavities?" I mumble, the dentist's fingers still filling up my mouth.

"Everything looks good, but you have bird poop on your pants."

I laugh because my dentist is the kind of man who takes his jokes very seriously and I don't want to risk it—the mouth is a sensitive place.

"I didn't see it a couple of minutes ago," he says. "Used to notice everything about everyone. Guess I'm starting to unravel."

"You're still the only man I trust." I hear my words then probably turn red. The dentist shouldn't matter so much to me, but he is a certain age and a certain type of man, so he does. I sit up to rinse out my mouth. I'm not surprised by the blood, but when I scan down to the white-and-green splotch of bird crap on my knee, my voice gets too big for a family business, "Motherfucker!"

The dentist rises gracefully and goes to the door, peers around the corner, then closes it extra gently. He's a very good businessman. Probably a very good father.

"We'll just clean you up a little then you'll be all set."

"And the blood?"

The dentist smiles very slowly, trying not to hurt my feelings. "Just some inflammation."

"The flat canines?"

"Like I said, you're still grinding at night. There's nothing more to it. For a couple hundred bucks you can get a real nice guard that'll last longer than you can live."

"Well, that all depends," I say, then I cut myself off with a tight smile that says, *We're done here, I recognize you have other appointments. My time is up.* But inside my head I carry through with a rant, defensively siding with Shira's denial, that one can ever stop existing.

On my way out the dentist shakes my hand one last time and says, "See you in six months and in the meantime, watch out for birds."
I laugh just the right amount.

When I get home there's a small box at the door. I step over it and go inside so our neighbors can't hear me. I call up the number and start yelling. I think I say something like, "You capital-hunting whores, you money-fuckers, you life-sucking sluts," but before I can get nice and worked up in a way that feels satisfying, another call comes in, so I switch over just in case, because you never know who might be trying to reach you.

It's Shira and she says she'll be home late tonight, if at all, but she wants to know if the electric toothbrush arrived. I say yes and thank you very much, it's just what I needed, and if it weren't for you, I'd have forgotten my age was changing this week.

Shira says it's amazing we used to live under the same roof all those years as little ones, never stopping to think what it was like, and now we're adults and we can stop anytime to think about anything, but we never want to.

"Anything that exists," I say.

"Exactly. Anything." She uses her I'm-a-seventh-grade-teacher tone to bring the conversation to an unambiguous end.

I brush my teeth. My thoughts spin around with the toothbrush head until I pause on a childhood memory of Shira walking in the bathroom just as I reached the moment of no return, my face contorted, toes scrunched up, torso twisting and all that muscle and flesh she was never supposed to see. Later that night a steady rain tapered off and the black sky faded into dull greens and yellows. A high-pitched siren went off so we crammed with our parents into the least cluttered corner of the basement. My thigh and forearm pressed against Shira. This may have been the last straw, the one that forced our family north and east.

An unexpected, undocumented storm caught them between islands. In a few hours they would have anchored then cooked up fish and rice for an early dinner, played a game of gin rummy and then hit the hay before rising with the sun and saying to each other, "Those kids of ours really missed out this time," and then sailing back to the mainland to return up north to their amorphous city, unnavigable to visitors, where both of their children had apartments and jobs, but nothing holding it in place, nothing keeping it from slipping into the Atlantic. The next day they'd be back in their offices with all that beautiful vacation inside them. But the wind spun the boat around, the bow and stern trading places. The boom swung relentlessly at their heads. No time to take down the jib. Let the main sail do what it wants. You better, or else. On the radio, static. All static. Oh, here's something, nope, just one distant reggae beat. They deserted the helm and flung themselves into the cabin where a deck of cards and paper plates littered the floor. For the time being, they could stay warm and dry in there.

And then it must have ended like this: at the top of the sea, the waves played catch with the boat before finally swallowing it whole leaving nothing to see, nothing to touch, nothing further to examine.

Then Shira and I tried to live in the middle of the country, but sometimes we'd confuse the big sky and distant horizon with the vastness of the sea. One day we were driving on a road that never turned and would never have ended, mostly flat grazing land to the sides, an occasional cornfield, which felt better, the stalks taller than our car, but they were seasonal and flimsy and we could drive right through them. The mountains, though, they would stand their ground.

Shira is on a sixth date with a man whose name has the same number of letters as mine, but as usual she won't tell me anything else about him.

In a couple of weeks, Shira's age will change to thirty-five. I call to make an order. A man with whom Shira would want to live, a soulmate, someone who likes children, and doesn't give too much credit to statistics. Not angry, not too kind, not too rich, not too gentle, not in love with an ex-girlfriend, not registered on Second Life, not a user of Google Earth, not a beach lover, not someone who thinks too concretely, not lachrymose, not a completely unfamiliar face. Eyes the color of land.

"Sorry, bud. We can get almost anything these days, but we haven't been approved yet to deal in humans."

"That's fine," I say. "It'd be hard to make a person just appear."

"You'd be surprised. We're getting there," he says. "Anything else I can get for you today?"

"How about bird poop?" I joke.

But the man starts to enter the order and asks about quantity, color, consistency and delivery location.

"Does it come from an actual bird?" I ask.

"At some point it did."

I hear voices out front, so I say *nevermind, no thank you,* end the call and go to my bedroom window, which looks out over the street. Shira and a man lean against a small round car the color of smoke or murky water. The man's hair is longer and curlier than mine. It moves when he moves, when he smiles, when he talks. His nose is smaller than mine, but similar in shape and slope and his clothes fit his body as though they were wearing him. But when the man finally edges closer to Shira and turns to face her so it's really just him and her, Shira, who's taller than most women but shorter than some, stands on her tiptoes so she becomes taller than this man, then reaches around the back of his head and pulls him into her neck, rubbing his back in circles, patting the back of his neck and probably saying something like, "It's going to be okay, it's impossible to lose something." She pulls out her phone and makes her screen light up then sends the man back to where he came from.

Tonight the time will change. We'll lose an hour, but we don't really lose anything. We won't feel a thing. Simply, time won't move forward for an hour. We'll be sleeping and then when we wake up our phones and computers will have pretended that nothing happened.

But when the time changes or rather stays put, I happen to be awake because my gums feel funny, as if they're being scooped out of my mouth.

I find myself with eyes closed in the bathroom rinsing out my mouth with warm water, which awakens my bladder, which awakens all of me, and then I feel some pressure in my boxers that I let myself attend to, but after just a couple pleasurable movements I notice my teeth clenched, my face warm and red, and I can only think of limbs being pulled off bodies, cars crashing into other cars, and entire cities burning. I find myself with hands squeezing biceps, breath held, and sweat dripping from my forehead down my nose and onto my upper lip when I hear the young couple who live in the other half of our house cheering long and hard as though they'd won the lottery. But they're not the type to play the lottery. They have a Boston Terrier, their practice child, they call her. I think of yelling through the wall, "Congratulations!" But Shira sleeps lightly, so I just listen. The cheering fades into normal conversation, and then an abrupt silence. Still, I wait. Once it's clear they won't talk the rest of the night, I floss, then brush, then try to figure out the time.

"So when do they hurt the most?" the dentist asks.

"At night," I say. "But that might just be when I notice."

The dentist tilts back my head and shines a light into my mouth. He pulls my lower lip down then my upper lip up and then he casually mentions he'll need to take an X-ray.

"We'll cover up all your important parts," he chuckles and puts heavy pads over my groin, heart, and neck.

It's hard to believe that sometimes everything goes right and two people make another person, and more often than not, despite all that can go wrong, people just keep living the way they always have.

"You're slowly losing mass in your gums," the dentist says. He holds up the X-ray against a lit-up whiteboard so I can agree with him.

"Goddamn them," I whisper. "What now?"

"Lots of flossing and massage your gums with an electric toothbrush." He checks his watch and touches his jaw gently. "That should help delay things."

The dentist reaches out to shake my hand and send me off to his wife at the front desk to make a follow-up appointment so we can continue to monitor the rate of recession. The dentist's hand is warm and heavy and cozy like a wool blanket, and so I hold onto it a little too long.

•

There's a fidgety young man at our door. He might be a teenager. A navy suit hangs loosely from his bony frame. More than his age, his hair catches me off guard—blond, straight and gelled. So do his tiny nose and pinned-back ears. Eyes the color of our bad dreams. "We don't want any," I say. I'm ready to tell him he needs to take a good hard look in the mirror and make some serious decisions for himself. But before I can do this, I feel Shira's hand on my back.

Shira wears a sleeveless red dress that hits right below the knee. A swooping cowl neck, a pair of dangling turquoise earrings, and silver strappy sandals with a slender heel. An oddly shaped pendant, also silver, swings at her chest. The entire outfit is new to me.

"Know how to get there?" Shira says.

I start to answer, "I have no goddamn clue," but the young man cuts me off. "Don't need to," he says. "Have a lady in a box who tells me every time I need to turn." He laughs a little, amused by the way he's described common technology.

Shira covers up her hesitation with a closed-mouth smile and offers her arm to the young man before she can change her mind.

In his car, low to the ground, they start to go one way, and then they do a three-point turn and speed off towards the highway.

Our neighbors are on the other side of the lawn waiting for their dog to finish urinating. From my hip, I give a little wave, which they don't notice, and then I mosey towards them, but the dog finishes and they drop to their knees to smother him with hugs and kisses.

At Shabbat services, there is an impressive wart on an old man's ear. When we stand, this old man a row in front of us, who will soon die of something close enough to "natural causes," remains sitting. I catch myself estimating the diameter of the wart while he and his hunched over wife, who is just barely able to stand, and Shira, wearing a snug purple dress, and the rabbi, whose job it is to remain close to the center, and everyone else, whose eyes I feel on my shoulders because they are broad and powerful like a swimmer's, but naked without tallit, chant together seamlessly as though they're one person. The wart is round and rises off the back of his ear and takes up space that didn't belong to this man before the wart came along and claimed it.

I'm surprised we're here, and I'm even more surprised it was my idea since I was kicked out of Hebrew school at ten for something I said, something about the rabbi's face lacking symmetry. This is a place I can easily make fun of, a place Shira will only defend if I mock the concepts our parents argued over, salvation and afterlife. But I figure we can stand to meet some people we just might recognize.

The old man clears his throat and chokes on a bubble of saliva. The eyes of the congregation shift to him and then onto Shira's dress, which is the second brightest thing to the stained glass window in the room. The man coughs and Shira extends her arm to pat his upper back. I turn swiftly to sneer at her. My kippah falls to the floor. Before I can get nice and red having to bend over and pick up the little cap and then pop back up admitting my recklessness, the prayer comes to an end, and all but a few sit for the next one, the Mourner's Kaddish, for those who have lost someone in the last year.

It's unclear if Shira means to stay standing. Perhaps she's caught in a daydream. Maybe she's mesmerized by the old man's wart. Or she needs to stretch out her back and legs, wants to show off her dress to the men and women behind us; the path her body takes is easy to follow. But when I look up, her eyes are not on the wart. Her lips move but not with the prayer. The space she takes up is more than usual. Her hips and elbows are unapologetic, not reeled in, her head bobs. She is alone, the only stander in our row. One row up prays the old man's wife. One row back, a lachrymose middle-aged woman. When the last words are chanted, Shira is not unaware. She retreats gracefully from her stance and whispers to me, "Ready when you are," her face calm and relieved.

I don't see it, but on Shira's shrill command I swerve out of its way or at least hope I do. We're only three blocks south and five blocks west of our house. In the rearview mirror, no sign of blood or guts. Up above it's too cloudy to make certain of anything but clouds, though the mountains surely have not left us.

"It was much smaller and rounder than a cat," Shira says.

"Did it have a bunch of legs?" I ask eagerly.

"More than four?"

"Maybe we should go back," I say. "Just in case it's someone's pet."

"There'd be no way of knowing," Shira says. "Just get us home."

We creep by a middle-aged couple on a leisurely walk, holding hands loosely, two fingers each, looking in opposite directions. I slow down so much they stop walking and turn towards the street, expecting us to roll down the window and ask for help. But once I get a clear look at their faces, content and yet uncomfortable, I hit the accelerator a little too hard and drive home where two boxes the width and depth of canoes, one as tall as Shira, the other my height, block our entryway.

"What'd you get me?" I ask. I feel my face heating up, ready to say some harsh but well-intentioned words. *We can't keep ordering stuff for ourselves, for each other. This is not healthy. It's indirect.*

"I don't know," Shira says, turning red, her eyes avoiding the boxes. "At this point, I'm really not sure."

There is no sign of a receipt or return address. On top of the shorter box, there are a few dime-sized holes. Shira hangs back. The neighbors fling open their door and argue over who left a wet towel on the floor while their dog runs laps around the yard. They seem not to notice the boxes or us, and for a moment I let myself wonder if we and the boxes are actually there to be noticed.

With my hip and then my shoulder, I nudge the box that's about my height. It easily stands its ground. To my surprise, the box's surface is much warmer than the cool fall air. I put my ear to it and think I hear sniffing and a familiar sigh.

"Thank you," I say to Shira and then I wrap my arms around the box and squeeze, knowing I'm likely getting my hopes up. I must be smiling because I feel my gums collapsing under my bottom row of teeth. Shira waits until the neighbors go inside then comes over and puts her hand on my back where it is flat and firm. She says, "We ought to get these open."

Year of Jesus

The first time Geoff passed through Effingham—reveling in memories from his college days while humming along to Dylan, Liza drifting in and out of sleep in the passenger seat—he simply missed his exit, which he didn't realize until the massive cross popped into view.

Ten, fifteen, maybe twenty stories tall. A pristine white structure, nothing around it, not even a McDonalds, as if it grew straight out of the ground like an indigenous plant. When he tried to get back to his light-hearted college memories (late night buffalo chicken calzones, the Christkwanzikah party, public urination, Ping-Pong), it was too late because the cross made him agitated and he could only think of how he used to have tons of friends and now he had only a few.

And then the bitter feeling must have stayed with him through the Kaplan family Hanukkah party because he got into it with Cousin Scott at a volume such that a majority of the seventy guests had no choice but to bear witness to his most pedantic and condescending register, the one he'd reserved for internal monologue and his nuclear family. It didn't matter that he was on the right side of history and Scott was ignorant at best—for the remainder of the party all the relatives spoke to him with an extra layer of politeness, but evaded topics of substance. It also didn't help that as soon as they left Cousin Whoever's finished basement way out in the burbs and climbed into the old station wagon, his parents and sister agreed that Scott meant well.

Now that he was alone—nine turbulent months since discovering the Effingham cross—he purposely drove thirty minutes out of the way. Liza would have objected. She wouldn't have agreed to even an extra five minutes on the road, especially not to peek a giant cross. He supposed his family would feel the same way. They weren't religious, but they lit candles on Friday night, never ate pork, and didn't feel comfortable around visual representations of Christianity that weren't at least a few hundred years old.

He enjoyed the drive from Chicago to St. Louis to visit his family. The road remained flat and turnless. He could practically fall asleep without consequence. Cornstalks stood straight and still, indifferent, casting a golden sparkle. He liked having nothing to do, not being physically able to do anything but drive. These days work was particularly busy. His company had been making personnel cuts, which meant longer hours and doing financial things he didn't know how to do, things he said he knew how to do in his interview because he knew Professor Google and Professor YouTube would be there for him when the time came. Soon, once the dust settled with the divorce, he would look for a new job, perhaps even a new career. He would devise a plan to get back on pace, catch back up to his peers, and he would finally take the plunge into the open mic scene.

He was working on a joke about couples who grocery shop together when the cross came into view. He remained in the fast lane but slowed down to about fifty as drivers sped by and then cut right back into his lane, too socialized by downstate politeness to give him anything more than an annoyed glance.

It was just as he'd remembered it. Tall. White. Alone. Made by humans. Probably loved by some, hated by others. Kind of like me, he thought, and chuckled to himself, tapping the break. He wanted to get closer to the cross, perhaps even touch it—it was alluring—but somehow that would feel wrong, taking it too far, betraying his family.

The cross shrinking in his rearview mirror, he conjured up the joke he had been working on just a minute ago. The punch line was that one member of the couple always emerged as the hero of the shopping trip, usually the person who remembered to buy toilet paper. He hadn't particularly enjoyed grocery shopping with Liza, but now, perhaps for fear of unwanted nostalgia, he'd been ordering his groceries online.

He exited Highway 40 at the world's largest Amoco sign, barreled down Skinker Boulevard and turned onto his quiet, tree-lined childhood street. The neighborhood had recently voted to open the Skinker gates.

The sister and the brother-in-law and the baby were waiting for him in the front yard. They were wonderful—weren't they? The kind of family that everyone wanted to be around. Attractive. Positive. Energetic. Not too pushy. Not too passive. Oozing health and vitality. Intelligent but not dogmatic.

So why could he no longer stand them? He couldn't put his finger on it. The brother-in-law's contentment? Her ageless glow? His positivity? Her unconditional support for family members? He could have murdered someone and she would have visited him in jail and said that sometimes people simply needed to use murder as a coping mechanism and that he should accept and forgive himself. Or was it that they always brought little gifts? The ease at which he changed a diaper? Their enthusiasm for his divorce? They had loved Liza, they were so happy at his wedding, had made a joint toast that convinced even him that he and Liza were meant to be. Now, just like that, they agreed Liza wasn't right for him, and without provocation the sister boasted that she would unfriend Liza on Facebook in a heartbeat, if that's what Geoff wanted.

The sister handed Geoff the baby and the brother-in-law wheeled his little black carry-on bag up to the front door.

"Jacob missed you," said the sister. "Didn't you miss your Uncle Geoffy? Don't you just love your Uncle Geoffy?" She looked up at Geoff. "Isn't he the cutest?"

"Hey little man," Geoff said, rubbing his nose against the baby's nose. It was soft and smelled sweet.

In the kitchen the parents each gave Geoff a big hug and then everyone gathered around the breakfast room table over a bowl of overripe peach slices from Grandma Edith's weekly produce drop off.

Yesterday morning they met with Liza's family rabbi in the northern burbs and made their split official. They snuck in the divorce just in time for Rosh Hashanah, the New Year, which must have appeared symbolically motivated and therefore made good sense to Geoff's family, though he didn't have much to do with when it happened. It was Liza's idea, but he was willing to go along with it because why would he want to be with someone who didn't feel like herself around him? Those were the words he needed to hear; the ones that made him realize why he sometimes found himself holding his breath during broad daylight or woke in the middle of the night from grinding his teeth.

"It's so good to see you, Geoffy," said the mom. "I like your haircut."

"Very handsome," said the dad.

"Agreed," said the sister, "I like it short."

"Thanks. I'm flaunting my ears. Bringing back my fifth-grade style. I even bought a six-pack of Umbros on eBay."

The brother-in-law offered a chuckle.

"What about the ones in your dresser?" said the mom. "You don't need new ones, do you? You should really clear out your room sometime."

"He's joshing," said the brother-in-law.

"I love it, our in-house comedian," said the mom. "Speaking of houses, Geoffy, guess who bought the Lerner's house?"

"Do I get a clue?"

"She's an old friend of yours."

"Really? I was never friends with girls."

"A friend," said the sister, using air quotes.

"Just tell him already, he's losing interest," said the dad, chewing and shaking his head.

"Her husband's a hotshot lawyer. He was on the Ferguson case," said the mom.

"Which side was he on?"

"Oh I don't know. But he's a really nice guy."

"Valerie Strong?"

"First guess!"

"Well, I didn't have that many friends," Geoff said, borrowing his sister's air quotes.

"I didn't know she was a friend," said the dad, proudly.

"Didn't last long, but we were good friends for a month or so."

"That's the best kind of friend," said the brother-in-law.

"This family's in the gutter," said the sister. "Jacob's not having any friends until college, right honey?" She rubbed the baby's forehead.

"Let's talk about the news," Geoff said, suddenly embarrassed, but also wanting to steal a moment to remember the excitement that Valerie Strong's seventeen-year-old lips ignited inside of him. It was like nothing he had felt in the last decade. "Anyone read any news today?" He looked around the table and everyone including his seven-month-old nephew seemed to be annoyed by his question.

"So you still trying the comedy thing?" said the brother-in-law, and then everyone seemed to relax, if not perk up.

"Yeah, tell us some jokes," said the sister.

"It's really just for fun," Geoff said, but he was happy to have a willing audience. Liza usually claimed to be too exhausted or too untrained or too close to the material to give Geoff any feedback after he would hold her captive in front of his stand-up routine in their living room. He reached into his pocket and touched his little notebook.

"I bet you're good," said the mom.

"He's got great timing," said the dad.

Now he no longer felt the urge to perform. His parents' affirmation still had an inverse effect on him.

"Maybe tomorrow," he said, letting his notebook remain in his pocket, "I just drove five and a half hours."

"You must be exhausted," said the dad. "Let him take a nap."

"We do it in under five hours," said the mom. "By the way, Geoffy, I want you to take this stack of mail. All these credit card companies, I don't know how they find you here, but some of these are good deals. You can get fifty thousand miles on Delta just for signing up! You can always cancel."

"Or I could just marry a pilot," Geoff said.

The dad laughed out loud and everyone else commented that his joke was funny.

"Hey, what about the apples?" said the brother-in-law. He'd converted for the sister and already knew more about Jewish traditions than anyone in the family. Apples for Rosh Hashanah was mainstream knowledge, but the brother-in-law had studied the stories of Purim and Hanukkah and the more obscure holidays. He also read Hebrew fluidly, and his blog, *Jew-bies*, had been written up in the *Jewish Light* and averaged one hundred and seventeen unique visitors a day.

"You're totally right!" said the mom. "Our in-house Rabbi. Don't you just love it?" she said to the sister and the sister nodded, part embarrassed, part proud.

The mom sliced up apples and poured honey into a colorful ceramic bowl they had brought home from a market in Guatemala or Costa Rica, Geoff couldn't remember which.

"Happy New Year!" everyone called out as they bumped raised apple slices held between sticky fingers.

"To capitalism," Geoff said, and the sister rolled her eyes.

"La shana tova," said the brother-in-law, and everyone smiled, repeating the Hebrew phrase as if they were in an intro language class.

That night they hurried through Shabbat dinner, delayed by the brother-in-law insisting he perform the full Kiddish while donning his custom-made yarmulke. Then they piled into the beige 1993 Honda station wagon, which the parents kept around because there was no need to replace it. They drove ten miles west on Highway 40, and pulled into a subdivision made up of large mid-century ranch houses.

"Fifteen minutes to get anywhere in St. Louis, isn't it great?" said the mom, turning back to look at Geoff. Perhaps she saw his divorce as an opportunity to realize her dream of the nuclear family being together for all occasions. He'd be lying if he said he hadn't considered moving back, his childhood home was still a comforting thought when he was away from it, but ultimately it felt like a step backwards and he was desperately trying to move forward, or at least stay in place. After all, his fifteen-year high school reunion was in two months.

The street was parked up so they drove down to the circle and tried to park on the curving part of the road. The brother-in-law, still wearing his yarmulke, eagerly hopped out to help the dad maneuver closer to the curb.

"So many friends," said the dad, shaking his head in disbelief and yanking up the parking break.

"We were lucky to have been invited into Leonard's world," said the mom.

They walked around the side of the house and into the backyard. Easily a hundred guests gathered around the pool and under the covered patio. A handful of kids played on the grassy slope between the pool and the brown picket fence. There were passed hors d'oeuvres and a full bar and a projector playing a slideshow of Leonard and family on various vacations.

The brother-in-law claimed a pool chair and the baby soon fell asleep on his chest. Strangers came over and ogled the sleeping baby. He truly was adorable, more so than most babies, but Geoff wouldn't admit this to his sister because why should it have mattered? The parents were quickly drawn into conversation with a couple that looked familiar to Geoff and the sister went inside to find a bathroom. He could hear his mom over the chorus of party noises talking about how her grandchild was such an easy baby: "He's just so adaptable!"

Geoff promised the brother-in-law he would get him a whiskey. He snaked through to the bar, taking any opening he could get, but still grazing legs, brushing arms, and bumping butts. He was fourth or fifth or sixth in line, it was impossible to say who was in line, when he reached high for a mini crab cake, and jostled someone's drink.

"So sorry," Geoff said, putting the entire appetizer into his mouth.

"No worries," said the woman whose drink he jostled. "Hey, is that you Geoff Kaplan? No way—it's been forever!"

He turned to meet eyes with Molly, Leonard's youngest daughter. She wore a white Panama hat high on her head with a navy ribbon around it. He didn't know Molly well, hadn't seen her in a good ten years or so, but had noticed on Facebook that she was keen on wide-brimmed hats.

They caught up quickly. She worked in finance, had two kids, her husband was somewhere over there. He also worked in finance, but did something very different than her, she emphasized. She loved living in St. Louis, so much less hassle than Chicago and so amazing to have family around as a built-in support system and babysitters! Then she went on mini rants about St. Louis humidity and public schools and started on one about certain neighborhoods changing. Geoff felt the euphemistic potential for the word *changing*, so he decided to get right back into small talk; he couldn't afford to lose his cool in this setting. He'd most likely damaged his relationship with Cousin Scott beyond repair. The silver lining, however, was that after the blowup—incited by Scott's insistence that Darren Wilson must have had a very real feeling that Michael Brown would have killed him if he didn't kill Michael Brown first—Liza had suggested Geoff try to convert his outrage into something productive like protesting or volunteering. Later that week he tried out for the Orange Bananas, a long form improv troupe, something he'd been on the cusp of doing since he landed in Chicago after college, ten years prior.

"How are your parents?" Geoff said, cutting off Molly.

Molly tilted her head back as if someone had attempted to spit on her, made an excuse about needing to check on her mom, and then disappeared into the crowd.

Was his non sequitur that abrasive? Or perhaps Molly's exit had nothing to do with him. Maybe she simply didn't like him. Everyone wasn't going to like him, which was something he had to accept. But as Molly pushed through the crowd, he glanced at her smooth calves and felt a pang of doom in his stomach.

He and the brother-in-law sipped whiskeys on the pool chairs and pulled down appetizers as they floated by. Leonard's wife stood on the diving board and called for everyone's attention. She began by toasting to her husband's sixty-seventh birthday. Geoff would have liked to see Leonard's reaction to his wife's heartfelt words, but he couldn't locate him. A minute into the toast Geoff started to really listen and grasp the wife's usage of the past tense and looked around and noticed dozens of tearful eyes, and then came a vague memory of his mom telling him some bad news about a friend. It was during the roughest patch with Liza, when his parents still hadn't known they were anything but head over heels for each other, and his brain would dance around during conversations, unable to process or retain much. It was indeed a birthday party for a dead man, and yet, it was the nicest birthday party he'd ever attended. His face hot with embarrassment, he started to count the number of guests, but stopped when he hit thirty, having only made a small dent in the crowd.

The next morning, while the family went to synagogue for Rosh Hashanah services, Geoff stayed home, drank two cups of coffee, and then took a stroll around the neighborhood. The houses were large brick colonials with two-car garages and thoughtfully landscaped lawns. He never noticed how big they were as a kid; they were just the size that houses were. He wasn't monastic, wasn't ready to ditch it all for a tiny house, but unlike his sister he didn't aspire to live in a neighborhood like the one he grew up in.

At thirty-three, he was the age his dad was when they moved into this neighborhood. The seriousness that now flowed through his veins seemed to have come out of nowhere. He didn't remember feeling it at twenty-nine or thirty or even thirty-one when he hadn't yet had a ten-year college reunion, his Facebook newsfeed wasn't yet crowded with baby pics, and none of his friends had gotten divorced. About a year ago, Emily Millstein, one of Liza's dear friends from college, called Liza to let her know she and Ben were splitting up. "I just don't get it," Liza said, having announced the news to Geoff over dinner. "We were just at their wedding like yesterday." Throughout the next few months, during dinner, on walks, in bed, on the L, Liza continued to bring up Emily Millstein and how she just couldn't wrap her head around it. And then one day she said she did get it, had probably got it all along, which was probably why she was so fixated on not getting it, the implication of getting it terrified her, but better to get it now than getting it after getting a baby.

Though all the houses were way bigger than anyone needed, the Lerner's appeared especially grand with its pillars and balconies and slate roof. It was hard to imagine his contemporary setting up shop in there. On a couch in Valerie Strong's basement where they were "studying for an exam" between rounds of shirtless, quasi-pleasurable friction making, she had told him she wanted to be a professional dancer and if that didn't work out, then she would do graphic design. He must have told her he wanted to be a lawyer so that he could help people not get taken advantage of or discriminated against, surely by then he'd already given up on his musical and athletic aspirations.

Now outside Valerie Strong's new house, a sold sign with the realtor's proud face on it pegged into the front yard, he pulled up her profile on Facebook. They weren't friends, so he couldn't see anything but a thumbnail of Valerie Strong and a blond toddler kissing her on the cheek. He quickly powered off his phone and started thinking up a new joke. For all Valerie Strong knew he was indeed a lawyer, the good kind, if she ever happened to think of him.

He didn't know how long he was standing there scribbling in his notebook. The joke was about millennials, how they were now buying up houses in teams on their parents' streets and dividing them into apartments, where they would set up Etsy shops and drive for Uber and run an Airbnb and whatever other random things people were doing to make enough bucks to keep afloat.

"I heard this one went for over a mil," said a man's voice.

Snapped out of thought, Geoff turned to see a couple about his parents age and a hyper poodle. The man wore a faded Cardinals hat and had vestiges of black hair in his sideburns and down his neck. The woman wore fitted jeans and a thin white turtleneck. She had remarkable posture, which made Geoff straighten out his.

"Makes me feel great about our place," said the man, "might be able to get eight hundred for it, and just think, we bought it back in '79 for one-eighty."

"If only he would agree to redo the kitchen," said the woman. "Let's put this to rest now: Geoff, would you and your wife buy a house with wood trimmed countertops and cabinets? Not to mention ancient appliances."

The couple looked familiar, but he couldn't place them. The good news was that it didn't matter because he could always feign familiarity—it was a social skill he had developed at a young age, as he and his sister got paraded around to his parents' friends' gatherings where they were often the only kids.

"Honestly, I don't think I'll ever buy a house," Geoff said.

"Not with that attitude," said the man.

"What difference does it make to you?" said the woman to her husband.

"During the first few years you'll worry about every tiny blemish, but then you'll loosen up and you'll get so comfortable it becomes like your own flesh and bones. But then how are you supposed to part ways with it?" He looked to his wife, expectantly.

"Oh, right," said the woman, smiling, "says the guy who still inspects the tiniest scratch on our wood floors, so tiny you'd need a microscope to see it. You'll feel relieved once it happens. A little sad, but relieved."

"In case you're interested," said the man, bringing his voice down to just above a whisper, "ours is going on the market soon. The space is too much for us and we don't want to deal with stairs now that we're moving into our so-called golden years."

"They live out of town," said the woman, embarrassed, "you knew that."

"We're in Chicago," Geoff said. His use of the plural pronoun felt dirty.

"Great town, though too much traffic for me," said the man. "And I can only imagine your heat bill."

"You would have gotten used to it," said the woman to her husband, frowning. "Anyway, say hello to your parents for us. We see them walking all the time. Your dad loves Ellie." She bent down to pet the poodle's head. "And your mom always brags about you."

"That's my mom," Geoff said, curious as to what exactly it was that she was reporting.

He watched the couple stroll side by side down the sloping part of the street, the stretch that made his calves burn when he used to race Thomas Murphy up it on his bike. For a moment the couple was holding hands and Geoff found himself unable to look away. Then Ellie became interested in a squirrel and pulled the woman into someone's freshly cut yard. Geoff exhaled and decided he better be home to greet

the family when they got back from synagogue because that's the kind
of family they were.

When the family came home from synagogue everyone looked
exhausted, but no one went upstairs to rest. They seemed both happy
and surprised to see Geoff, as if they had expected him to have
absconded or curled up in bed. Everyone kicked off their shoes and
plopped down on the couches. Geoff did the same, comforted by their
presence; it was nice having people around.

"How about some iced tea?" said the mom. "I have fresh mint
from the garden."

Everyone agreed that iced tea was an excellent idea.

"Do some comedy for us, Geoffy," said the sister. "We need to be
entertained after that sermon."

"You have no attention span!" said the brother-in-law, squeezing
the sister's shoulder. "That was one of his best."

The sister rolled her eyes.

The baby made a squealing noise followed by a burst of laughter
while pulling on the ears of his stuffed dog.

"See, even your nephew wants jokes," said the sister, "he's laughing in anticipation."

"Don't pressure him," said the mom, "but we'd love to hear what
you're working on."

"Only if you want to," said the dad.

Geoff wasn't particularly funny and he knew it. Comedy was just
a hobby. But he would continue to fantasize about getting so famous
from telling jokes that high school classmates would line up for auto-
graphs at his twenty-year reunion. These fantasies calmed him even
more than swimming or mediation or sex.

This was his family, though he sometimes didn't feel it, they were
the people he remained closest to, so he couldn't just lay himself bare
or they might get concerned or offended. He'd warm up and feel them
out with the non-personal and take it from there.

"A new study shows," he started up, pleased that everyone was looking at him, "that twenty-five percent of Italy's tourism has been referred by American pizza boxes."

A long, dangling second of silence and then the dad offered a laugh.

"Huh?" said the sister, looking at the brother-in-law for an explanation.

"I get it," said the mom, "very funny."

"We never eat pizza," said the brother-in-law, "your sister won't let us."

"Fair enough, I'll try another one. Did you hear about the man who built a house inside Walmart?"

Everyone shook their heads *no*.

"The man goes around the store gathering materials, finds a space in the back of the store and builds a tiny house. A few days later, the store manager comes by with a box of Entenmann's donuts and welcomes him to the neighborhood."

"Oh, that's good!" said the dad. "You really can get anything at Walmart. And it's so big, you truly could build a house in there!"

He could feel the others melting into the couch. He needed something that would snap them upright and onto the edge of those tattered cushions, the same cushions he used to pretend were linebackers and spin off of with a Nerf football tucked under his arm.

"You used to make jokes about me being a man," said the sister. "Remember? Those were so funny!"

"I truly doubt that," Geoff said.

"You did. You used to sing a song about me actually being a man. Dad, you remember, right?"

"Sure, sure. I was a homosexual in that same song."

"That's right! And you had Grandma Edith having sexual relations with her cat." said the sister. "It would make our sides cramp up."

"My sense of humor has evolved," Geoff said. He couldn't believe he was that kind of teenager, but he did remember the song, he even remembered the unsophisticated tune.

"Do one more," said the mom. "It's not so different from tennis, you have to warm up to get in a groove."

"Not everything is tennis," said the sister.

"One more! One more! One more!" chanted the brother-in-law.

"Alright, alright," Geoff said, but he was feeling defeated. At best the dad found him mildly funny. Maybe it was his delivery, or maybe his family simply wasn't his audience, or maybe he truly wasn't very funny, which was okay, but it also wasn't okay. He needed a subject they were invested in.

"I don't know if you all noticed, but the demographics in affluent suburban America are really changing. The baby boomers are retiring and selling their big multi-story houses and moving into condos. No stairs, no lawns, no maintenance."

"It's true," the mom blurted out, "but your dad and I aren't going anywhere anytime soon."

"Let him finish," said the dad.

"So anyway, you'd expect young doctors and lawyers and business people to buy up these beautiful old houses in the best school districts, but there's a different group of people outbidding them."

"Really?" said the mom, concerned.

"Valerie Strong and her lawyer husband are the exception."

"I hope not," said the sister.

"Teams of Millennials of six, seven, eight, sometimes as many as fifteen are buying one house."

"No way," said the mom, "there must be laws against that."

"It's true. And each house is brewing beer, renting out a room on Airbnb, selling handmade jewelry and hand-curated thrift store clothes on Etsy, and involved in multiple Kickstarter campaigns." He exhaled and paused. "Hashtag New American Dream."

The brother-in-law laughed, but he would laugh at any joke that referenced Twitter because it was important to him to let people know he was active on social media now that he was a blogger.

"You're so natural," said the dad, "you deliver just like the pros with all the pauses and inflections and gestures."

"Wonderful, Geoffy," said the mom. "I can totally see how funny you'd be to people your age."

But the sister and brother-in-law, who were only a few years

younger than Geoff, had busied themselves with making silly faces
and animal sounds for the baby.

"I don't know where you come up with this stuff—you're really too
much!" the mom added.

Why didn't anyone ever tell the cold, hard, honest truth in his
family? The years of affirmation had made him feel as though he would
coast through life achieving everything he set out to achieve and within
his desired time frame.

"Are we still going to the zoo?" said the sister. "Jacob hasn't seen
the baby elephant yet!"

"Did you know he was born at 230 pounds?" said the dad.

"And you complained about seven and a half pounds," said the
brother-in-law to the sister.

Both of the parents laughed heartily. Then everyone but Geoff and
the mom hurried upstairs to change into their *zoo clothes*.

"This must be hard," said the mom. "But you have plenty of time."

"I guess," Geoff said, "or maybe there are different models."

The mom stared at Geoff, waiting for him to say more, to open up
into a monologue featuring all his worries and struggles and need to be
comforted, so she could inject more affirmation and positivity into his
psyche. But it was a new year in which he would embrace discomfort
and uncertainty. He took out his phone and read out loud the forecast
for the week, knowing it would serve as an adequate distraction. "Perfect tennis weather," he concluded, and then the brother-in-law came
bucking down the stairs making pig noises with the baby bouncing on
his shoulders and giggling. The mom glided over to her grandson with
open arms and a barrage of kisses.

Ironically, Geoff thought, while at the zoo he had never felt so much
like an animal in captivity. The crowds closing in on him, the inescap-
able smells of shit (though not his own) and fried food, and then there
was his family who seemed to be viewing him with the same intrigue
as a gorilla—appreciating his uncannily familiar behavior yet privately
hoping to witness something exotic, if not perverse.

While the family ogled a sleeping polar bear and tried to convince a restless baby that it was worth waiting because *Mr. Polar Bear might wake up any second now,* Geoff excused himself and started on the two-mile walk back to the house.

He took the most direct route, which meant getting yelled at by a golfer whose green he cut through, darting across Skinker sans help from a traffic light, and passing behind Valerie Strong's new house via the alleyway.

He stopped to admire the back of Valerie Strong's house—to get a fuller picture of what her life would be like? Making a visor with his hands he peaked through the gate's wood panels; he couldn't see much, but he could tell the yard was large and overgrown by neighborhood standards. Trying to widen his view, he pressed his face against the gate and it clicked open. He nudged it further so that he could now see the driveway and an old pine tree and a brick patio with a black metal table and matching chairs. He couldn't help himself. He entered the property, gently closed the gate behind him and strolled up to the patio. His legs were tired from all the walking, so he took a seat.

He closed his eyes and tried to recreate the nervous excitement he felt the first time he hung out alone with Valerie Strong, the current of anticipation even more electric than that of touch. The sun, the walk, the family, the memory, must have worn him out because as much as he resisted, his thoughts became increasingly fragmented and blurry.

He woke to the sound of a car door shutting. By the time he opened his eyes and realized where he was, there was a short and clean-cut, mildly attractive man in his thirties standing over him.

"Hey buddy," said the man, "How you doing?"

Geoff squinted and offered a meek *hey man.*

"Sleep well?"

Geoff studied the man. His bangs were pushed back with a pinch of gel, and his blue eyes were neither kind nor unkind. He wore a black polo shirt tucked into jeans. Gray running shoes. No immediate reason to make a run for it, so Geoff eased himself up, but his foot had fallen asleep.

"Don't get up for me," said the man, taking a step back and scrutinizing Geoff.

"Sorry, pins and needles," Geoff said, shaking out his foot. Because he was taller than the man, he was careful not to stand up too straight. "Your place?"

"Now wait a minute—it's not your place?"

"Nope, I'm trespassing."

"No way—me too! I've always admired this neighborhood, so sometimes I go for Saturday strolls through backyards and live vicariously. You too?"

"I'd be careful, man." He didn't look like the trespassing type, but nonetheless, Geoff was relieved. "The yard signs around here don't always match up with the way people act. You know, like, when push comes to shove."

"I'm just messing with you, buddy. Wifey and I closed on this place a couple of weeks ago. Doing a few renos then moving in next month."

So this was Valerie Strong's husband. Geoff was now self-conscious of his muddy flip-flops, unclipped toenails, lime-green hoodie featuring coffee-stained drawstrings, bushy eyebrows, and worn jeans. He tried to come up with a joke, but all he could think of was the very real and very true fact that this man either prosecuted or defended Darren Wilson.

"Congrats on the house," Geoff said, looking deep into the lawyer's eyes but coming up with nothing either incriminating or vindicating. "And sorry about all this."

"You're fine, you're totally fine. In fact, glad someone's getting some use out of the patio while it's still nice out, ha-ha. Though, I would like to know why you're in my backyard? It's pretty weird, man. I mean, you tell me if it isn't a little weird."

What was he supposed to say? Didn't people sometimes peer into other people's yards? Didn't the voyeur upon occasion find himself in said yard? Sometimes he might even fall asleep on a patio chair. Wasn't it a matter of odds that every now and then this series of events would play out? And so here they were.

Geoff only shrugged.

"So I really don't want to make this a thing, but my wife and daughter are in the car and I want to be one hundred and ten sure that this isn't going to happen again. We bought this house because of the neighborhood, so we wouldn't have to deal with anymore unexpected encounters now with a kid, and of course the school district. So help me understand why I got a call from a neighbor on the one Saturday in a million years that I'm not working. Maybe you live down the street and were just a little curious? I'm sure you can imagine how this little situation could be a little disheartening."

Geoff was suddenly annoyed at whoever was responsible for making the call. He looked over at the nearest neighbor's house and noticed a part in a second-floor curtain and a sliver of a face. Having money made one mistrustful; his parents' over-sensitive alarm system was case in point. Growing up there wasn't a single attempted break-in, but the alarm had been set off many times over the years by the flickering flame of a Shabbat candle, a meandering birthday balloon, a bill sliding off the breakfast room table. *Better safe than sorry*, the mom would say, waiting by the phone for the alarm company to call to find out if they needed to send over the police.

"Sorry, man," Geoff said. He considered naming a *dangerous* part of the city as his place of residence, but no way he'd be able to pull it off. "I'm in from Chicago." He thought about adding that he was visiting his parents who lived down the street, but then Valerie Strong could easily put two and two together, and more importantly, he didn't feel compelled to assuage the lawyer's anxiety.

"Great town, even if a little rough in parts. I have a cousin in Evanston. Kind of like here but with the lake. By the way, I didn't catch your name."

"William," Geoff said. It was the first name that came to mind, and also happened to be the name of Valerie Strong's senior year prom date. He wondered what William Edwards was up to these days.

"Alright, Will, I'm going with my gut here. You look super tired, but you don't look like someone who's up to shady activities. Actually, you look a lot like one of my brother's friends. You happen to be related to any Goldberg's?"

Now there was too much trust between them. Why should the lawyer get to feel so at ease? Why should Geoff feel so unthreatened in a stranger's backyard? Either everyone should be threatening to everyone, or no one to no one. Geoff looked up at where the neighbor had been peering through the curtain and then over at an old oak and then down at his largest arm mole of which three coarse hairs were sprouting out of like a bouquet of flowers. There had to be a joke somewhere.

"Wait, you said you're a lawyer, right?" Geoff said.

The man nodded then shook his head. "Did I mention that?"

"So I have this friend," Geoff started up, no idea where his joke was going, but pleased that the lawyer's face had tensed. "And he does one of these new family heritage DNA tests that are now all the rage. He's one of these guys who's really into his—"

Geoff paused at the sound of a car door closing followed by the emergence of a woman, squirming child in arms, cautiously shuffling up the driveway and calling out: "Andrew." Geoff wished he could become invisible so he could stick around and see Valerie Strong, even if for a fleeting second. But the millisecond before he and she would have shared a moment of recognition, he spun around and strutted, his very best cool guy strut, through the back gate and into the alley, the lawyer calling after him: *Hey man! Will? What's your deal? William?! What the fuck?!*

The family was already home. They didn't ask where he'd been even though at least two hours had passed since he left the zoo. Instead, they massaged his shoulders and brought him iced tea and dropped the baby into his lap, and asked him what he wanted for dinner—he could have anything he wanted.

That night, hunched over bowls of the dad's famous chili, the mom mentioned they ran into the Eisner's as the zoo and Paul Eisner, who ran an advertising firm, was looking for fresh talent at the entry level.

"Your creativity would transfer nicely," she said.

"It's entry level," Geoff said, shaking his head. They'd had this conversation many times over the last ten years; the parents had a million friends and so there was always someone hiring.

The mom smiled as if Geoff said he would gladly consider the job, perhaps because this time he said nothing about it being in St. Louis.

"Sorry about Leonard," Geoff said, pleased at how seamlessly he had diffused attention.

"Thanks, honey," said the mom. "Did we tell you how it happened?"

"He doesn't need to hear that now," said the dad.

"It's disturbing," said the sister, "really creepy."

"Well now I need to know."

"It's making me upset," said the dad. "These freak things are much scarier than cancer. You don't even have a minute to look it in the eye."

"You have to tell me," Geoff said.

"Another time," said the mom. "It's the New Year, we're supposed to be celebrating."

"Let's enjoy this little cuddle bug while he's still little," said the sister, cupping her hands around the baby's face. "How cute is he?"

"He's alright," said the brother in law, shrugging, which incited a roar of laughter from the parents.

After dinner, in the final rounds of a heated Scrabble game, the phone rang. Even though everyone shouted at the mom to let it ring and finish her turn, she popped up and grabbed the landline off its base. She said nothing after her initial hello, and shushed the family into silence, the phone pressed tight against her ear. After hanging up, she went over to the back door and double locked it, flipped on the fog lights out back, then told the family that the call was an automated message from the police reporting one or more trespassers in one or more backyards on their street.

"I told you we should have voted against opening the Skinker gates," said the dad.

"Well, now we'll have to have a revote," said the mom.

"So creepy," said the sister. "Now I'm going to worry about you guys. Maybe you should think about a condo."

Fighting back a grin, Geoff shook his head and grimaced and commented that the neighborhood just wasn't what it used to be. Everyone, even the baby, seemed pleased with his contribution.

Rules

Because it was after midnight, she insisted he walk her home. She knew the way. He was new to the neighborhood, the town, the state, the Central Time Zone. In the last month, several women had been attacked. A few men, too. Minutes ago, she had been on the ground. It was wet so she slipped. And then trying to help her up, he slipped too. On the ground, she tickled his stomach. He laughed then rolled out of her reach and sprang up. She rose slowly. They had danced that night. Just a little. He worked for her, officially. She was a Manager, he was a Coordinator. She came up to his chin. He needed glasses but preferred to maintain his look. She asked about his pay, and he told her without hesitation. She then cut her stride in half. She had been a rower in college and still worked out at the gym. Most considered him athletic because of his BMI, but he never played for a team, not even Little League. His parents preached cerebral development. Her family ventured out on ten-mile hikes and fifty-mile bike rides. He was an only child. She had a younger sister who had just made an announcement. The sister had loved to say how she was unsure about marriage, but she didn't want to wait forever, so she dithered to a yes and then immediately and emphatically leaked the news. He slowed down too. He felt it rude to walk ahead, even half a stride. He asked her how she liked it in this little city, and she said it could be worse but it could be a lot better, and though it was aesthetically unimpressive, the people were nice, they wore nice expressions and said nice things to others and often did nice things for others. The attacks were fluky, she said. Just people forgetting the rules for a split second. He wanted to ask what she meant, but he didn't want to start a new conversation, so he thanked her for taking him under her wing those first couple of weeks, showing him the ropes, giving him a night out, being a friend.

It didn't matter that she was a Manager or that three of the last five people she kissed were women; the way he hugged the inside edge of the sidewalk brushing a neighbor's fence with his puffy jacket suggested she had been closing in on him, filling in space. And here he was, a tall and slender man, taking control seamlessly, instinctually, subconsciously. Consciously. He now walked a quarter of a stride ahead of her. Of course she was used to this—a man trying to create physical space. And yet she'd done the same to men but would never dare do it so subtly. That would be wrong. She had told herself she would yell or run if it came to that. If she felt an unwanted wandering hand slide from side to hip to butt, she would jerk away and laugh a little to give him a chance to pretend nothing happened. But on a first date last year, when the hand returned and felt forcefully planted—she and her date, a friend of a friend of a friend, were on a dark side street—she'd began to consider her options and froze up. When he pulled her into him and slid a few fingers beneath the waistline of her jeans, she should have spun out of his grip, but instead she ended up under him, her warm body on cold sidewalk, her foggy head on damp grass.

This man, though, her co-worker, would be a perfect gentleman. As long as he didn't push her to the ground, he was free to do as he pleased. He could keep walking half a stride ahead, chin pointed up, arms swinging. She knew he didn't have to worry how that looked. And so for a split second, before the fence ran out, which was sharp and rusty, she too forgot the rules. With uncalculated force she used her rowing muscles to fill in the space between them; he used his instincts to protect his eyes and brain. The fence's metal bars didn't rattle the slightest when he slammed into them. He clutched his shoulder, eased himself down to the moist cracked-up sidewalk and lay on his back taking long slow breaths. Surprised, with a cupped palm she pushed her breath back into her mouth. The creak of a door swinging open came from a nearby house. Then footsteps onto a wood porch. She shuffled back in the direction of her apartment. Propped up on his elbows he looked up and down and across the street. She offered him a confused look as if she were on a late night stroll and had just stumbled upon a man on the ground. Biting his lower lip, he offered an embarrassed grin. Her entire body felt like it was shaking. She shuffled over to him and bent down, sort of amazed by what she had done. She waited for his grin to shrink then gripped his hand and pulled. He did his part, pushing off his feet. First they heard a siren in the distance, probably over in the student neighborhood, then a dog barking, the creak of the door, footsteps onto the wood porch and a woman on the phone. Once the siren came closer, they started jogging, soon after they picked it up to a brisk trot and then a near sprint. For a while they ran next to each other down the middle of the street as if they were in lanes four and five on a track. He ran hard and awkwardly, on his heels, out of breath. She ran with ease on the front of her feet, pumping her arms and kicking out her legs. When she noticed he was no longer at her side, she stopped and looked back only to see the silhouette of a man with his hands on top of his head, the lights of a police car closing in. Surely he could explain himself, she decided, then she started running again. She pushed off her toes and lifted her knees high as if she was being chased; no one would suspect otherwise.

Zeros and Ones

Our bellies are full of Easter, mine for the first time. I wonder what Neal is thinking. He likes to start and finish his thoughts with silence. I do the opposite. Neither of us is eager to be alone together even though a week has passed and what happened could have happened to any two housemates, any two best friends, any two men in their late twenties. Just by chance, just that one time, just for the sake of not being all or nothing.

Neal's mom, Beverly she has us call her, is driving us back to Boston. We don't have a car and Beverly says buses are dangerous these days, too many have flipped over or caught on fire. But I think it's that she wants to spend more time with Neal. There are four of us in the front of her slim pickup truck. I'm folded up into three quarters of a man.

"Who do you like better, short people or tall people?" Adrian, Neal's little brother, wants to know. Neal is talking even less these days, so I answer, "Short people," though I'm the tall one.

Beverly glances beyond Adrian and sees two male figures who for many years have not been boys but who also don't live like men. She glances a second time in search of a clue, because these days Neal will only offer one or two words at a time. Maybe she notices the physical space between us, an inch we've managed to create out of nothing, but what could that possibly let on? She looks again and rests her eyes on Neal's emerging beard, a length of facial hair he has never attempted. "Makes you look distinguished," Beverly says, letting the car drift across a lane of traffic.

The blaring horn of an eighteen-wheeler jolts us out of our private thoughts. I pop out of my seat, my head stopped by the ceiling. Beverly yanks the wheel and swerves back into our original lane. Adrian squeals then pushes out a string of staccato breaths. I find my hand clutching Adrian's knee and quickly pull it back hoping it wasn't there too long. Neal stares blankly at the road in front of us. He has no reason to react to a *near* accident. What's done is done, and what will happen will happen. What's avoided is avoided.

We pass a sign that reads "Worcester 25, Boston 68" and our vehicle starts going much faster. Beverly seems of no particular age. She went to college on a swimming scholarship but dropped out and married when Neal started growing inside her.

"Do you like brown grass or green grass better?" Adrian is only nine but weighs as much as Neal. His flesh flattens against my left side.

Beverly's frizzy hair blows into her mouth then she sighs and rolls up the window for a quarter of a song on the radio before she can't take it anymore, rolls it back down, then lights up a Merit.

"Brown grass or green grass?" Adrian demands an answer.

I want to take back some of what I said at Easter dinner, but I also want to say more. "Brown grass," I finally say.

Adrian looks satisfied with me then turns to Neal. "What about you, Neal?"

Neal only shrugs.

I wonder if Adrian is testing us—his questions could easily be metaphors. Now I worry I chose wrong. I was just trying to have fun, right? Go against the grain, to see what happens. "Actually, I like green grass better," I say, but no one seems to hear me.

The road curves right, and now I'm pressed against Neal. His oblique holds its ground and digs into my side. I wish he were softer.

"Brown or green? Green or brown?" Adrian shifts in his seat pushing me further into Neal and Neal further into the window.

"Yeah, yeah," Neal finally says, "I prefer concrete."

"The guest makes the toast," Neal's dad said. "That's how it works at the Caraker house."

I used simple words like "Grateful, wonderful, together, special, family, delicious, feast," but without knowing it, I left out a few words everyone was expecting to hear. Neal's dad popped up, thanked me, and finished what I started. I should have been silent and gracious, but that's not the way I work when there is more to say, so I jumped up and resumed center stage to the clinking of glasses. "I want to thank you all again for having me." Out of the corner of my eye I could see Neal's clenched jaw telling me to wrap it up and sit down before I let on too much, before I made Easter about something it's not, but I needed to admit to *something.* "And what else can I say other than"—I looked to Neal's dad's girlfriend for empathy, a short Guatemalan woman who during the kid's egg hunt had politely answered a series of questions about Mexico from Neal's grandma—but she was looking down at her plate of ham and green bean casserole and scalloped potatoes. "This is my first Easter," I announced. Blank faces turned into jumpy eyes and gentle smiles. "And it's even better than Passover!" A couple of chuckles. "And I have a hole in my sock." Roars of laughter. "And once I peed in a Gatorade bottle because I was too lazy to walk all the way to the bathroom." One pity laugh. "Just one room away," I added. A collective sigh. *And I masturbated in my grandma's living room. And the synagogue bathroom. And I thought about people way younger than me and some way older and some in this very room. And I've never physically harmed anyone, well, not a human being, but sometimes I imagine a situation in which I do. And sometimes I consider stepping in front of a bus so I can face the inevitable on my own terms. And I cheated on every single assignment in my college computer science class. The only concept I bothered to learn was binary. The simplest of them all.*

•

There are four urinals at the rest stop bathroom but Adrian pulls up next to me. Neal hangs back by the sinks. Adrian finishes first. While I shake off those lingering drops, Neal whispers to Adrian. I turn my head slightly but can only make out a phrase here and there, "not polite . . . too crowded . . . that guy."

On the way back to the truck, Adrian asks Neal, "Who do you like better, Mom or Dad?"

"Beverly," Neal answers automatically.

Adrian frowns and waits for an explanation.

Our legs are stiff, our upper bodies sore, so we zigzag back to the truck delaying things as much as possible. We pass a group of three men and two women, wearing UCONN sweatshirts and hats, leaning against a blue Escort missing a couple of hubcaps. They share one cigarette and flirt with each other in all sorts of different combinations.

"I like them both," Neal says forcefully. He then softens his tone, "For different reasons."

Back on the highway the blue Escort flies by us, smoke billowing from its tail pipe, arms dangling out the windows, indie rock blasting. I think of our trip to Montreal back when we were in college. A bunch of us went up in our friend's minivan with only our wallets and winter coats. We popped in and out of shops, flipping through racks of shirts we found intriguing but would never buy. We drank dozens of Labatt Blue and finished the night at the casino hemorrhaging what little money we had. We kept saying stupid things like, *What happens in Canadia stays in Canadia* and *Spring Break 1997, woot woot,* even though it was November of 2001. At the casino I lent Neal fifty bucks because his parents still received his bank statement, and he didn't want them to find out he'd been in Montreal. Neal had been talking to his parents less and less as it was becoming clear they were talking to each other less and less. He wasn't trying to keep secrets, but he wasn't going out of his way to keep them updated. He didn't want them to keep him updated. On the way home we pulled off the road and slept in the van, using each other's shoulders as pillows, our breaths musty, our clothes sweaty and stuck to our backs. We were drunk and exhausted and a bit dejected from losing all of our money at roulette.

But we woke up in good moods, content to be heading back to our little bubble where together we ate and slept and wrote papers and made love to our girlfriends, not realizing that one day in the near future many of us would drift to different corners of the country, buying houses and making families with people whom we'd yet to meet.

Adrian grins at the speeding Escort and says, "What do you like better, going fast or going slow?"

"It depends," I say.

Adrian nods. He does not care what it depends on. He just wants both of us to answer his question.

"Neal?"

"It depends," Neal agrees.

Adrian continues to grin. He is amused by our answers.

Beverly eases up on the accelerator, and the back of the blue Escort disappears around the bend.

Back in our college days, Neal and I lived in one of the smallest doubles on campus. I dated Rachel and he dated Cynthia, roommates who lived in one of the largest rooms on campus. They pushed their beds together to create separate quarters for sleeping and studying. Neal and I figured doing the same might open up our space, so we did and it did.

Later that day we played Wiffle ball on the quad. After a couple of games, the other boys gulped down Gatorade in the student union while Neal and I lay in the grass. I revealed my recently acquired fear of death as if I was the first person to recognize our non-permanence. "You're no different from anyone else," Neal assured me. I laughed, then said, "That's not even close to true." The sun in his eyes, Neal only squinted. "We're full of disparity!" I declared, but I wasn't sure if that was the right word or if I was even responding to him. The brewing of the clipped grass, damp soil and our sweaty backs emanated a rich earthy odor that reminded me of what I had recently discovered under Rachel's jeans. Neal patted my thigh and forced a smile. I must have amused him. But he in his coolness, in the way he never bothered to worry about the things that make us or don't make us, filled me with an urge to do something I'd never done. I waited for a pack of off-balanced frat boys to pass, then rolled onto Neal's stomach, pinning his hands above his head with my hands and his thighs down with my thigh, elbows with elbows. A bead of sweat rolled off my cheek onto his lip. "You're so goddamn calm," I avoided shouting, not wanting to draw any extra attention. Neal only breathed. I shifted so our bodies aligned with each other in a way that felt both pleasant and painful. I kept him there. I occasionally shifted to feel more friction, but ultimately the lack of movement, with all that potential, became too much, as if holding your breath. The others emerged onto the quad, refreshed and ready to start up again. We let our bodies untangle and pretended we were just boys being boys, but later in his steadiest, coolest voice, he said, "You better sleep with one eye open tonight."

We left the beds together. To move them we would have had to acknowledge certain things. But when Rachel and Cynthia finally saw the arrangement, Rachel forced out a throaty laugh and Cynthia said, "Very funny, guys." And then, before we headed out to dinner, Rachel insisted we separate the beds, "In case we get back late and you're too tired."

"What's Jewish?" Adrian looks to Neal.

Beverly's phone rings. She checks her screen, smiles and then leans on the accelerator. Neal clamps his mouth shut and nods. I think of the woman who showed up during dessert and hung back from the adults, haphazardly watching the kids hunt for eggs between short intense glances at Beverly. We blaze through Framingham. Not a single car passes us. My left side tingles. My right side aches.

"Are you Jewish, Neal?"

Beverly shakes her head as though she's made some terrible mistakes and they're finally affecting the well-being of others. "It's not good to ask so many questions, hon."

These questions are nothing, I think. They're not metaphors. They fill time and space and that's it. They spew from a nine-year-old-boy's mouth, a boy who eats too much junk food and plays too many video games, who arrived eighteen years after his brother, who has every right to be curious until—

"Am I Jewish?" Adrian interrupts my thought.

The gentle curve of the exit ramp is enough to send Adrian into me and me into Neal. I now remember the way Neal's hip bone dug into my thigh and how mine must have dug into his. I can't blame him for what happened. We're free, between girlfriends, have enough money, an entire city to run around, yet we've been this way for years with no one to obsess over, no one to make decisions for or with. All it took was a late night in the living room, a few beers, another round of our perpetual argument over which city had the best baseball fans, followed by a particular silence; me pinning him down like that day on the quad, excited and frustrated, not knowing which feeling to follow. "I could really stand to hurt you," I said. Neal's silence was inviting and assured me we could try something new and never have to talk about it.

"Short people," Neal says. "I like short people better than tall people." The question was asked back on I-95 over an hour ago, but I'm the only one who recognizes how this answer could matter.

We hurry through the narrow, winding streets of Boston, just barely avoiding other cars and pedestrians. Beverly speeds past our split-family house before she uses her entire body to brake and flip the truck around. Neal and I untangle and drop out of the cab. Neal limps around the driver's side and hugs Beverly with one arm. She mostly talks and he mostly nods. Finally, Neal says, "Keep an eye on that one," pointing the crown of his head at Adrian.

Beverly looks at Adrian and must wonder when exactly she'll start to know him less. She then looks at Neal and must wonder when he became a stranger. If only she could pinpoint the moment. "You look tired," she says, then waits for Neal to respond, but he just scratches his beard. "I hope you're having some fun, not working too much. Letting yourself live." She waits again, but Neal only nods. "Take good care of yourself." Beverly's statements are more posed as questions. *Are you tired? Are you having fun? Are you taking care of yourself? What the heck are you up to?* Neal continues to nod, sending Beverly back to the truck, unsatisfied, returning home empty-handed. As she opens the door, I blurt out, "We're taking good care of each other."

Beverly slings her arm over the door. She looks both eager and willing to wait as long as it takes. She must want to know, *How exactly do you take care of each other?*

I slap my hand onto the back of Neal's neck. I can't see his face because I'm intent on looking Beverly in the eye, but I can feel his body tighten up, holding his breath, waiting for this moment to pass. "We go out on weekends and cook during the week. Plenty of veggies," I say. Beverly gives me a grateful smile. "We introduce each other to all kinds of new people." Beverly shuffles closer to us, her eyebrows raised. "Sometimes we have a drink or two and there's some horsing around." Neal exhales and I find myself squeezing his shoulder. "Sometimes we get a little rowdy," I add.

I bite my tongue and squeeze Neal's shoulder harder, as if wringing out a wet towel. I feel my fingers digging into muscle, not wanting to stop at bone.

Beverly's smile fades.

Neal doesn't move. To react would be to reveal. Still I wonder what his silence means. I wonder if he himself knows.

Beverly crosses her arms over her chest and narrows her eyes.

"What's going on out there?" Adrian shouts from the truck.

This is an excellent question. My hand starts to cramp up, but it's either this or saying more, so I smile and tighten my grip.

"Are you hurting him?" Beverly says, lighting up a cigarette. Neal's face must be bright red and contorted.

I wonder if I'm hurting him.

"Beverly," Neal says softly, but she doesn't hear him.

He takes a deep breath. My brain clicks back on. He sighs and my hand goes limp and falls from his small shoulder. I frown at Beverly and think to mutter the words "I'm sorry," but nothing comes out. I'm not sure these are the right words. So I just stand there trying to decide whether to feel proud or guilty. If only one of these options felt true.

"You're still just boys," Beverly says, mostly to herself.

"Mom," Neal says. "He wasn't hurting me."

Beverly takes a long drag from her unlit cigarette. "Right," she says, reaching into her jean pocket and fumbling for a lighter. "He's practically family."

Neal won't reply. He won't utter another word. He won't say what we are because words like *friend* and *family* and *lover* bleed into each other. He won't assure Beverly that they're still mother and son and always will be, and after many more years of growing apart, they will one day start to grow closer.

Neal and I idle over our unkempt lawn, willing a tree to fall or even a phone to ring. Beverly waits in the truck. She wants to make sure we get in. She wants to see which one of us opens our front door. She wants to peek inside. Neal scratches his beard, how he hates facial hair. I refuse to think what I sometimes think: *two men in their late twenties should not live together.* Adrian leans over Beverly and waves out the window, his pudgy hand flopping around like a fish washed to shore. Our neighbors are pulled out of their side of the house by a chocolate Lab. They seem older than us but younger than most people. They wear jeans and sweatshirts and always seem to be yawning. They keep to themselves, but we know sometimes they fight and sometimes they make love.

Will You Please Comply?

In a nature preserve outside Boston, a flash of lightning has set a patch of forest ablaze. Aaron has a view from across the lake of the fiery orange swallowing greens and browns. If there ever was a time for him to start avoiding risk, now is it, but he has covered more than half the loop, so going back the way he came, away from the fire, would only keep him longer in the woods.

Because the trail is peppered with roots and rocks and uneven patches of grass and mud, he lifts his knees higher than he would on the roads. Because he used to run races every weekend and win or nearly win many of them, he pumps loose fists beside his hips much faster than a jogger, the tips of his pointer fingers resting gently against the tips of his thumbs, *as if you're holding a potato chip and don't want it to break,* his high school coach had instructed. Because Nina will be induced in three days and her parents live two time zones away and his parent, his dad, has lost his mind, Aaron is just *walking in the park, then picking up ibuprofen at Walgreens. Home in forty-five minutes.*

He hears the rain patter against the treetops before he feels it on his neck and shoulders. He watches it poke hundreds, thousands of dime-sized holes in the lake's flat surface. It has been a few years now since he hit his physical peak. He didn't use to breathe so hard at such a pace. Now his knees need days off. So do his shins, his IT bands. In the mornings when he steps out of bed, he feels the weight of his entire body shoot through his feet. He uses the slick ground as an excuse to slow down and catch his breath. He has promised Nina to take it easy.

He hears a faint ringing in his left ear like a hearing test. He kicks his legs out quicker and further in front of him and thrusts his arms to match the turnover of his legs. From his track days, he has been conditioned. He runs as hard and relaxed as he can, dropping his shoulders, unclenching his jaw, the way he'd always been instructed. This is the two-minute drill, the bell lap. He breathes in slowly through his nose and then pushes out quickly and forcefully through his mouth. He rounds the final curve before he is on the same side of the lake as the fire.

The ringing stays with him, a constant and annoying sound. *If only I can ditch this head of mine. But what would I replace it with?* His dad replaced his head with a thing that hears and sees and smells and makes noises, but only unknowingly, involuntarily, uncontrollably, reflexively.

Aaron cannot see the fire, but when he looks up and out he sees streaks of smoke rising from the top of the woods. The rain picks up, and the ringing intensifies. He looks at his watch and is relieved to see only the amount of minutes and seconds he has been running. He tries to calculate his pace by rounding and dividing and then rounding, but he can't remember if the loop is three point one or three point five miles, and he's not sure how far he's gone, how much he has left.

Over the years, Aaron has lost a few things while running: keys, ten dollars, his driver's license. He assumes one day he will lose his ability to make decisions, the connection between brain and body. *Please put one foot in front of the other. Thank you very much.* He wonders if it will happen instantly or over many years. He doesn't know which he'd prefer.

He is not as far along in life as he sometimes thinks he is, though how could anyone know such a thing? He will color his hair for the first handful of years of his child's life, long enough for her to form solid memories. Running, he thinks, will either keep him going or set him back. He's seen it go both ways.

That morning he paced around the house cursing himself because he scorched the surface of a brand new frying pan, a late wedding gift. He had turned the wrong burner on, where the new pan shone without oil.

"Before you know it," Nina assured him, "the pan will be a few years old and will look how it's supposed to. No biggie."

He nodded because his wife made good sense, but he went back to the kitchen and held up the pan, grimacing at its black scars, orange and brown around the edges. Then he wrapped it in a plastic grocery bag and hid it in the depths of the pantry.

A red pickup with a flashing light on top is stretched across the trail. A middle-aged woman in green capris and a tan button-down shirt, a badge over the breast pocket, leans against the vehicle, her arms folded across her ribs, her hands tucked in her armpits.

Aaron stops running then stops his watch.

"Sorry, sir. This part is closed," the woman says.

"I'm just running one loop. I promise to stay on the trail."

"Sir, I'm just doing my job. Not trying to be unreasonable or nothing."

Until recently, perhaps until Nina became pregnant, Aaron hated being called sir. He remembered the first time it happened. He was in college, purchasing cereal and milk at the grocery store. "Paper or plastic, sir?" said the bagger. Aaron must have only looked at the boy because he, a boy only a few years younger than Aaron, repeated, "Sir, would you like paper or plastic?" The bagger sounded exasperated, the way a child gets waiting for his parent to wrap up a conversation with another adult.

The rain lets up so that now it's just a drizzle or maybe not raining at all. Aaron thinks the ringing is gone, but sometimes he feels a sensation that lingers even though it's not really there anymore, like when the stress fracture in his shin healed perfectly, but for months he swore the spot was pulsating like a heart. He figured the opposite could happen; a sound could stick in his head, and his mind would somehow dismiss it, even if it's very much real and external and can be heard by others.

"I need to take the most direct route home. My wife is pregnant," Aaron says. "I'm at Walgreens, you see? I'm not here. I can't be here much longer."

"Sir, you're in the woods and headed towards a pretty serious fire. You'll thank me when you turn on the news tonight. Trust me, these things can get out of control in no time."

"My wife is alone and in pain and ready to pop."

The woman turns and looks in the direction of the fire. "Then what in God's name are you doing out here?"

"Wanted to see how fast I could run around the lake. That's all."

"Sir, you can always come back another time."

Aaron knows he won't come back the next day or the day after, and probably not even in three or four weeks. He's tried to slow down and run casually, for exercise, for fun, socially, but it never works out. He gets bored and antsy and his legs feel like they're being held in place, punished, so eventually he rolls onto the front of his feet and lets his legs do whatever they want to do, settling into his fantasy: the home stretch, pulling up to the leader's shoulder, the course lined with screaming fans. No Nina, though. This is before Nina, before anyone ever needed him. Finally, a blast of adrenaline fills his body as he kicks by an old nemesis and lunges for the tape.

"Sir, I don't want to call for backup, but you're looking at me kind of funny. Will you please comply? Tell me you're gonna head back that way."

The woman extends her arm and points over Aaron's shoulder, down the stretch of muddy trail from where he had just emerged.

Aaron thinks five years back when he went to visit his dad and the den was filled with their collection of old Matchbox cars, some turned over, some alone in the corners of the room, some piled up like monster trucks. At dusk his dad changed into sweatpants and tall white socks. In the kitchen, with a running start he dropped down to the tile floor and kicked out his leg like he was sliding into second base. At dinner, a green bean fell from Aaron's fork onto the floor, and his dad laughed and laughed and laughed.

"Sir, will you please comply?" The woman steps backwards and glances at her truck.

Aaron feels a sharp pain deep inside his ear, and then the ringing returns. He gets on his toes, starts his watch and sprints past the truck; his legs spin like the blades of a fan. The woman yells after him to stop, to turn around, to be careful. Before she can decide to go after him or radio ahead, his toe catches a root and he goes down hard. With his wrists, he breaks the fall. He rolls, lies still on his back. His heart, he thinks, is taking up more space than usual; he can feel it throbbing in his back against the soggy ground. He doesn't remember making the decision to dart past the woman. From now on he will need to be more calculating. He pulls himself up, his torso bent forward, his palms brown with streaks of red. He takes a couple of wonky strides in the direction of the blaze and then stops. He sees the fire's orange glow, smells the burning branches, hears the crackling and popping leaves, tastes the wet and smoky air, feels its dragon's breath.

For a moment he stands grinning, enjoying his senses, admiring this glorious mess.

The ranger, now inside her truck, shouts out the window, "Just so you know, sir, I've called for backup. I didn't want to, but I think I gave you fair warning."

Aaron nods at the ranger, rotates the face of his watch towards the ground, and takes off running, back the way he came.

Permanent Condition

Leo put his toothbrush on the most critical and candid settings. He massaged his gums and reached for his molars, while a soothing female voice interrogated him, "What are you doing with your life? Will today finally be the day? You think you're up to the challenge?"

Even though he was only thirty-three and even though he believed it mostly didn't matter what anyone did, a good amount of the world's citizens would suffer terribly and a small amount would do just as they pleased, today he was particularly moved by his toothbrush's tone, which seemed genuinely concerned for his life's trajectory and his sense of self-worth. He looked out the window and down at the park and all its activity, over at one of the tallest buildings in the city, and decided it might still exist in one hundred years . . . two hundred years . . . forever? If forever was possible, then surely he could care about what he did today. He could care his way into doing something permanent, undestroyable.

He'd have to start with books. Reading them. You can't just go out and make a difference, knowing little to nothing about the world's problems. You can't just take your personal experiences and apply them to everyone else's, even those you think you're quite similar to. He'd seen others try this, but he didn't want to be like them. He had dignity and integrity and cultural sensitivity, and he didn't believe he was chosen to do any one particular task and didn't want to come across as didactic or pedantic; that was why he'd been so idle all his life, failing on three separate accounts to earn a degree from private liberal arts colleges.

A month ago, at Uncle Roy's house in the suburbs, during a party for his grandfather's ninety-third birthday, Leo pulled Uncle Roy, a hedge funder, and Uncle Stan, a patent lawyer, into a side room lit up by the glow of two slim computer monitors. Leo's PowerPoint presentation was vague and had only five slides, but it articulated that as an independent scholar, he was studying important issues that would make the world better for Roy's and Stan's grandchildren, if not their children. Without asking the hard questions, eager to get back to the festivities, Roy and Stan nodded along, shook hands with Leo, and agreed to fund him; surely they could write it off.

Leo's apartment was full of books he'd never read. It wasn't actually his apartment. It was his aunt's apartment who had been sent to Seoul. Preliminary studies showed there was a major Korean market for this particular type of electric toothbrush—the one that gave you positive and or negative feedback depending on the settings. While she was away, Leo was to collect mail and water plants and be ready to move out when she returned. She'd been away just a couple of weeks, and though Leo didn't want to return to his parents' house in the burbs, he'd yet to wander beyond Big Apple Grocery, only three blocks north. He talked himself out of hopping on the bus and exploring the city because he never had the right change and walking wasn't ideal because his lower back always tightened up after half a mile or so.

Most of the books had to do with improving the self. *Turning Inward at Fifty. Realizing Your Dreams and Then Actually Realizing Them. Playing Your Hand of Cards As a Woman in the Workplace. The Body and Mind As Individuals. Raising Yourself in Your Fifties.* Ah ha, here's something, he said to himself, *Call to Home: African Americans Reclaim the Rural South.* After five pages Leo became antsy, so he went to the park right in front of his building with a pen and notebook and approached a man watching after two kids.

"Sir, I'm a doctorate student in Socio-Cultural Anthropology at the University of Chicago and for my fieldwork I'm conducting a series of random interviews in public spaces in the city. Would you mind doing a short interview with me?"

"Sorry, man, sounds important, but my wife wouldn't approve of this," the man said, his eyes shifting between Leo and his kids, but his tone was inviting.

"I'm interested in the relationship between how Americans spend time and how they measure self-worth, happiness, etcetera."

Looking off in the distance towards the lake the man rubbed his bare chin and nodded. "I see," he finally said. "Know what, I'm at the park to watch my kids and at their age it's not an insignificant task, so you're better off talking to someone else." The man tilted his head up and went back to looking way beyond the park and his kids, beyond the lake.

"Of course," Leo said. "I certainly don't want to bother anyone, though I do think the work I'm doing is worth the bother."

The man now made firm eye contact with Leo. "Okay, well, I guess I do have something to say about your research topic. It's true I might be ten years older than you, but try not to think of me as a wise old man. Now this might not be profound, but I think it's worth saying. I'm not much of an intellectual, but I do like to think about these things. So here's what I have to say. I hope you can get some mileage out of it." The man exhaled and glanced at his kids. "Getting what you want is the worst and best thing that can happen to you because once you get what you want, you then have it, but you also realize that wasn't ever the problem."

"Interesting," Leo said, writing furiously in his notebook. "One more question and then I'll let you be. Does protecting your children from harm give you a sense of self-worth?"

"It keeps me from feeling lazy."

"And since you don't feel lazy, then you feel productive and therefore happy, confident, part of something bigger?"

"I didn't say any of that."

"Well?"

"I probably feel similar to how you feel about your research."

"Which is?"

"You know, a mixed bag."

"Thank you, sir. I'll be sure to keep you anonymous."

"Good luck. I admire what you people do. Digging, right?" The man laughed, walking away.

"In a sense," Leo called out, but the man was already out of earshot, scooping up his kids.

A week later, Leo conducted one more interview. Only Ricky the doorman had been willing to talk to him, and though he gave Leo an interesting perspective—being a doorman was plenty satisfying if one didn't obsess over what being a doorman did and didn't entail—after the interview Leo felt dejected and in need of fresh air.

On the roof of his aunt's twenty-two-story building, a young couple shared a bottle of wine and a plate of cheese and crackers. A tiny dog tied to the picnic table, nipped at their feet. Leo nodded at the man, who gave him a hesitant nod that said please don't get too close, I put a lot of effort into making this hour of our lives a long-lasting memory, or at least one hell of an hour.

Leo went out of his way to avoid the couple and arrive at the roof's ledge where he looked below at the park, down the shore at the swaying Hancock Tower and out at the white-capped lake, the little boats skimming the water's surface, impossible to tell at what speed. He wondered at what speed he would fall. Surely he wouldn't reach terminal velocity.

Leo kneeled on the ledge noticing a pair of silhouettes in a nearby apartment building looking in his direction, too far away to catch any of his facial details. He started to stand, and the little dog started to bark. Leo turned around, but the couple only looked at each other. It all felt too easy. He didn't want to go down in history as a man too introspective for his own good, who inevitably couldn't live with his own bottled up ambition, a man who always took the easy way out. And his family, there was some love there; you don't just go around handing out thousands of dollars to those you don't love and trust and admire.

The only way to find out how permanent something was, Leo reasoned, was to try to destroy it. He let himself think this, walking inches from the couple, now in an argument, and down the elevator to his temporary apartment on the seventh floor. A mind like this shouldn't have to splatter into pieces just to get noticed.

In the apartment Leo smelled a rubbery odor he hadn't been subjected to since his aunt left for Korea—the scent of the toothbrush, a ring of glue melding the body and the head. He noticed a few boxes in the corner adjacent to the potted tree and heard rustling in the bedroom. And then she emerged in a black suit, her eyes bloodshot and bugging out from flying around the world, too much caffeine, too much excitement.

"You're back," Leo said. "No luck with the Koreans?"

"No, they loved the toothbrushes, bought more than we can make. They're selling themselves. Literally. I'd go into a room with my special little guy and put him on the sales/marketing setting and then boom, ninety seconds later I'm collecting signatures."

"That's fantastic. Though I guess you have nothing to do now? Life is suddenly without meaning and direction."

"Oh heavens no! Now we're working on a computer that's able to give feedback on everything we do. Of course you can set it to be a yes woman or a negative Nancy if you're wanting to avoid the truth."

"What if you just want to hear your own thoughts? Can you program it to think like yourself?"

"What would be the point of that? You already have your brain doing that."

"Maybe it would be good to hear your thoughts from someone else. Might just scare you into trying new things."

"I don't think people want to try new things. Not unless someone tells them to."

"I agree. So the computer could have access to your thoughts and previous experiences and feelings about said previous experiences. Then it could devise a plan on how to proceed, which new things to try to ensure you are both growing and succeeding as an individual and contributing to the collective pot. Of course, it would have settings to account for cultural differences."

"You've always been quite the thinker, Leo. Why don't you write up a detailed proposal and I'll bring it to R and D first thing tomorrow? Maybe they'll want to bring you aboard. Also, we have to find you a new place to live, ASAP."

On the roof, Leo tried to stay up all night writing. His aunt said the proposal should be quite detailed and descriptive, but he didn't see what description had to do with anything. Meaning arrived in the form of feeling, and feeling was raw and human and brutal and difficult if not impossible to describe. It came from inside. There was little to see. Following that train of thought, he realized the computer would have to live physically inside the individual. It couldn't be seen or felt by the individual or the public. It would store its data on an external out-of-body-server so the individual could read and print feedback, and it must be able to give instantaneous feedback because, like with the toothbrush, that's what the masses sought. After a solid stretch of arduous thinking, Leo fell into a dreamless slumber. When he woke to the sun beating down on the back of his neck, he looked out, and as it must have done every day, he witnessed the city waking up. He opened his notebook and started to decipher his scribble. No, no, he thought. This can't be the solution. I'm compromising ideals for personal opportunity. There must be a way to make an honest living, achieve personal success, live a fulfilling life, have meaningful relationships with others.

Leo again looked out at the city and saw a few joggers shuffling through the park, cabs and buses blazing the freshly swept streets, and lights flicking on in the windows of tall buildings. *Who are all these people? What will they do today?* And then, just like that, willing to believe that some, if not all of these nameless people, were just as stifled by opportunity as he was, yet perhaps without the degree of introspection that tethered him to such a stagnant life, Leo stumbled upon his calling. "I've got it!" he shouted over the ledge of the building; one of the joggers looked up and then picked up his pace. *I'll help these people live meaningful lives and through this work I will find my meaning for myself. I'll be a life coach.* Leo snatched his notebook and flung it like a Frisbee; he watched it get taken by an air current and make various shifts and digressions before committing to a direction and finally descending onto a sunny patch of over-treated grass.

"I'm a life coach!"

Control

On the beach, my peripheral vision alerted me to the blond girl standing too close, staring at me with deep concern as if something ugly was oozing out of my head. She really was just a girl, ten at the oldest.

It had been fifteen years since I spent a summer teaching English classes to middle schoolers on this beautiful island where the Gulf funnels into the Caribbean, and for various reasons I hadn't returned since.

On a patch of warm sand next to my hip, I felt around and found the book I'd started on the airplane, *Imagined Communities: Reflections on the Origin and Spread of Nationalism*. I liked reading serious material on vacation—it was the only time I got any substance. If your job is to write daily blog posts with titles like, "Stop, Drop and Stretch: How to Salvage a Bad Run" or "Running Etiquette: do you throw snowballs and where are you from?" or "The Power of Casein Protein," then you inevitably start to get antsy and wonder if they'll ever allow you back into medicine. Maybe they'd let you work in geriatrics? I used the book to shield both the sun and the girl's eyes from my eyes.

You could have called it vacation, but most would have called it a honeymoon. Just as you could have called it a special commitment ceremony, but most would have called it a wedding. Of course no one called it anything now because our neighbor with a newborn had done his research, and even though it had been five years since my hearing, this neighbor felt the need to design and slip into mailboxes a glossy flier that didn't make me look so neighborly. I, too, wanted to protect the children, but this struck me as over the top. Sure, my thoughts weren't always what they were supposed to be, but whose were? And since the incident, I had become adept at slowing down the process of decision-making, letting impulses flatten and eventually fade out, not that the incident was anything more than wrong place wrong time. Regardless, my life partner to-be, a generous and compassionate woman, my soulmate, took her time to process the new information, then called off the ceremony but not necessarily our future together, which was understandable but had left me in a state of serious identity discomfort—a state I had left many a time before and hoped to have left for good. If I could explain why I let it happen, then maybe she wouldn't have felt I was now, just like that, a stranger. But how could I explain it to her if I couldn't explain it to myself? And unlike me, she didn't exactly believe that such a thing could just passively happen to an individual.

We were supposed to go to Puerto Rico for our honeymoon, but since I was now alone, I could go anywhere, and I wanted to go somewhere familiar, where I could feel nostalgia, spy on an old self.

The girl stood over me, touching the top of my head, gently knocking on it, to ask if anyone was home? A fair question. But my body ached and my head throbbed, so I didn't have it in me to escape this little tourist. I closed my eyes and prayed no one would get the wrong idea; some people were more susceptible than others to unfortunate circumstances, but still, I didn't feel sorry for myself.

I loved this island. It had been fifteen years since I'd been here. I hadn't wanted to go home that summer. The sinewy and touchy-feely Rogelio had offered me the extra room in his apartment and I said yes, willing to at least take a leave of absence from college, a setting where I faked it pretty hard to fit in. I didn't quite get how to lounge around in a group and know when to make the snarky comment or when to be sensitive, jovial, nerdy. I didn't want to know. These groups sucked you in, and before you knew it, you were programmed just the way they wanted you. The island also sucked people in. You'd think you were coming for a summer, or just a week's vacation, but you'd end up staying your entire life.

The girl wore a mango-colored bikini, a nice color for her complexion. She had retreated a few steps, her fingers no longer on my scalp. The tips of her wet hair settled nicely at the tops of her shoulders, which were getting a little red. She cupped her palms as if she was trapping a hermit crab and held them out in front of her chest, studying them, then the top of my head. I could have told her it's impolite and dangerous to stare at strangers, but I didn't find it worthwhile to guide our youth away from connecting with adults. I was not a dangerous man.

"You're bleeding," she said, then showed me the sample of blood she had been keeping in her hands.

I only nodded.

"I'll get my dad," the girl said. "He's strong enough to carry you somewhere."

She looked to the water where a shirtless man with a camouflaged baseball cap and a soul patch tossed a football with a little blond boy who stumbled backwards each time the ball smacked into his chest. Between tosses, the man tilted his head up and gazed down the beach and out to where the sea met the sky. The girl's little voice shouted for the man, but he had a beer, a football and a son to attend to.

She stuck her hands in my hair, sweeping it one way then back the other. It felt pretty good. I hadn't been touched by another human since the flight attendant tapped my shoulder to wake me up for the descent, and no serious touching since before the flier arrived in our mailbox.

"Yep, you're still bleeding. How'd it happen?"

I offered a shrug. The most I could afford to offer.

To my side there was my snorkel and my mask all scratched up. I had seen a barracuda snacking on the little fish who were snacking on the reef. Its nose pointed at me, showing off a long mouth of uneven yet razor-sharp teeth. I wasn't going to retreat because some aggressive being might or might not want me around. I was tired of having to leave places to accommodate others, so I swam towards it, and it, that judgy fish, darted into a cave. I dove down, peered into its hiding spot and saw nothing but blackness, thinking I'd wait. I'd just keep waiting. When I came up for air, I had been taken with the current and found myself in a ridiculous spot for a human being, tossed into some pretty hard and jagged rocks.

"On a scale of one to seven, how bad does it hurt?" the girl said. She squatted and like a slow windshield wiper passed her hand back and forth over my face. She paid close attention to my pupils.

It was funny being a doctor. You had your patient telling you one thing and the tests and your years of training telling you otherwise.

"You might have a concussion. It won't kill you. My mom sees them every day."

I turned around to find a woman on a towel propped up on her elbows, a best seller fanned out, her eyes following a heavily tattooed couple down by the water. I wondered if she saw what I saw, which was two people loosely holding hands, hoping for a sign that would make it clear if they should hold on tighter or make a run for it before it got too complicated. Either way, the girl's mom had little interest in us or her husband and son's game of catch, caught in that mental spot where the island ushered all of its visitors, where you must consider giving up everything you have for whatever you might stumble upon.

The girl kneeled down on my towel and put her hand on my forehead. She told me I felt warm and she'd like to take my temperature if she could get a thermometer from her mom who was a nurse and carried all kinds of medical stuff with her. She then flipped my hand over and put two fingers on my wrist. "It's good to check your vitals after an accident." This is where I had to draw the line. I had to say something or I might end up in a familiar place. All it takes is allowing the child to honk your nose or pull your ear, which you let her do because she's a little nervous being in a doctor's office, and then you laugh a little and she keeps going, and before you know it you're sitting on the examination table and she's moving around in your lap, squeezing your nose, pinching your cheeks, pulling your ears, breathing in your face, unaware of all that's going on under your clothes. You keep your hands to yourself, but you slide and readjust a little, your stethoscope bounces against your chest. You slide with just enough force, increasing the friction, the pain of your zipper pressing into you is welcome, you deserve pain, but it's not so much about the physical, you are letting this happen because she is smiling and giggling and you are making her day and you're not an active participant and would hate to actively squash her game. But it does feel good and you finally arrive in a state of euphoria, the friction bursting and shooting out into the world. You clench your mouth but can't keep a little yelp from escaping and for the shortest moment the only thing you know is that the walls are white, and then all of it, the friction, the euphoria, the pain rapidly dissolve and turn your body numb, your mind questioning every decision you've ever made or not made. The child, intrigued by your contorted face and fast breathing, asks what has happened and because you say you don't know, at home the child asks her parents what happened, and just like that, perhaps for the remainder of your life, you'll have to start thinking of yourself as someone you swear you are not; you'll have to move on and either keep secrets or let others render your identity.

The girl finally caught the man's attention and he trotted over with high knees, the football tucked under his arm, his pointer finger shoved into an empty beer bottle. "Don't touch his blood. Go over to Mommy," he said to the girl, then extended his arm so the bottle tapped the top of my head.

The girl stayed at my side, but the man didn't seem to care.

If I didn't already look like such a sad case, I'm sure he would have made me into one. Looking like shit had its advantages, and I wasn't going to pop up and wipe the sand and dirt off my face just so this man would feel comfortable putting dents in me. I didn't owe him an apology or an explanation. Hoping he'd realize he needed another beer, I closed my eyes and let my head droop.

"Wake up," the girl demanded, shaking me by the shoulders.

"Buddy, wake up," the man said, with so little urgency, I started to like him.

I opened my eyes but only because his voice reminded me of a good friend from med school—a man who juggled like a pro and always wanted to try Mexican and Ethiopian restaurants on the wrong side of town. He also liked to use the word "buddy." All those frat guys did.

"Look, buddy," he said, shoving his beer bottle into the sand, "let me take you for help. You don't look so hot."

When I tried to form words, I realized I hadn't spoken since ordering a ginger ale on the airplane. I even made it through customs and immigration by only pointing and nodding. I cleared my throat and tried again. "I'm not a tourist," I said. The words came out just fine, though my throat stung—I had probably swallowed a cup of salt water.

"I'm not either," the man said, then laughed a little. "Look, we should get going, before I change my mind." He waved to his wife and son, motioned to the girl with a firm hand to stay put, and then started packing up my things. I pushed his hand off my book.

"Easy, bud, I'm not ripping you off," he said, but I didn't care if he was. I didn't care if he was taking me to a private corner of the island to rough me up or even have me do things to him his wife wouldn't do. I really didn't care because to care would be to acknowledge that we have control over what happens. I just didn't want a boozy stranger touching my one possession that gave me a sense of what it was like for others.

He carried my bag and we walked down the beach at a pace much faster than I ever walked alone. The girl trotted to keep up, but he seemed not to care. "Look, bud, you're going to be fine, it really doesn't look so bad." He was eyeing one of those overpriced beach bars with swings for seats and a straw-thatched roof. "The truth is, I'm not being entirely selfless right now." He stopped and turned around. He made sure his wife wasn't looking. She wasn't, though the girl trailed within earshot. "I'm not going back to them." He swallowed hard and grinned like he had just successfully stolen something he wasn't sure he wanted.

"You'll go back," I said. "This euphoria, I know it. It doesn't last long."

"I'm not going back to them today at the beach, the hotel tonight. No way I fly home to Minneapolis on Saturday." The man picked up the pace.

"Look, buddy," I said. "I'm willing to grab a beer with you if you promise not to talk about this." I turned my head and saw the girl a ways back pumping her arms, her feet slipping in the sand, struggling to keep up with our long strides.

"Okay, but I'm not going back to them."

At the bar, he found another American in his forties with a goatee, impressive deltoids and an emerging paunch. The girl lay on her stomach facing us in a nice shady patch of sand under a palm tree ripe with little green coconuts. Her dad and the other man were quickly onto their second drink. The dad's new friend poked my stomach and leaned into me, "We're going to peel off the layers of the island. We're going off the beaten path to find us some real life, some freaky shit." His warm breath on my face felt like the sun. "You're coming with us, pal. We need a guy like you."

"What kind of guy is that?" I said.

"A guy who's not afraid to smash his head."

"A free spirit," the dad said.

"But what if I have a kid to take care of?" I said.

"C'mon, buddy," the dad said. "I saw how nervous you were around my little girl."

I tried my best not to look busted, yet I felt as if these men had read my neighbor's flier and were encouraged by it, excited even.

"Now look me in the eye and tell me you're a father," the girl's dad said.

"I'm not yet, but we're trying," I said, then backed away and onto the beach. We weren't trying, but we were planning to start soon after the ceremony. We were not young by child-making standards but both loved the idea of having someone else to love, someone who had to love us. The girl sprang up, perhaps thinking for just a second I was her dad, but even after recognizing it was me and locating her dad at the bar, she took a few generous steps in my direction. I picked up my pace without looking back until I arrived at the northern tip of the island.

I was surprised to encounter a modern hotel surrounded by pools and massage tables, and men and women in slim white shorts with tucked in white button-down shirts. They practically stood at attention. Where this hotel rose high above the rest of the island used to be a fenced-in pile of rubble from Hurricane Gilbert. Just like that, the island had moved on. I was relieved that a wasteland could grow into a beautiful modern structure, and happy to be among such cleanliness and order. I made eye contact with one of the hotel employees; I wanted to see if he'd let on any negative feeling about his employer, his uniform, the massive building, but he only looked at me concerned and apologetically as if to say, "If only I were allowed to help the helpless." Though he had me all wrong. I could still do whatever I wanted, but I wasn't sure

I could want the smallest thing—the wind to change direction, a plate of enchiladas—without feeling alone and selfish and wanting to share.

I kept walking, trying to avoid looking at any man, woman, child. I stopped and looked out at the sea. It was calm as always but rougher than usual. It did little for me. I kept walking. My Achilles started to feel loose and out of place. It had been wobbly and tender for a few months and the sand wasn't helping. But how could I feel sorry for myself? Most people had to deal with much worse. I stopped to watch a pelican descend from way up high, nearly taking the most direct route to the sea's surface, snagging a little fish or at least pretending to, titling its head back and twice swallowing.

From behind me, a pair of hands snuck under my armpits and cupped my pecs. It felt good in a painful sort of way. "Pinche Richard," said a deep familiar voice.

Whoever it was, he wouldn't let me go. He squeezed me and rubbed his prickly chin on the back of my neck. I didn't have it in me to put up a fight, so I inhaled through my nose then exhaled through my mouth and let my body go limp. Sometimes it just felt good to let others take on your weight. The man held me up, then spun me around so we were looking in each other's eyes. It was a familiar face, but he didn't look well.

"Rogelio?" I said.

"Getting old, my friend," he said, pointing to the streaks of gray above my sideburns.

He had always been lean but full of muscle. Now his cheeks took the most direct route to his chin, his biceps a similar width as his forearms, his head shaved down to stubble. Still he smiled earnestly like a child heading out to trick or treat. He punched my stomach and pinched my side. He loved to touch, and I had always let him do it. One time he just kept going and I let him. We were at his kitchen table playing dominoes, the shades drawn, and I stared into the black eyes of the monkey in the Frida Kahlo portrait above the fish tank. "For the experience," he said. "For the experience," I agreed. And then I just let it happen; one of his hands working on me, his other hand directing my hand up and down on him. We finished, and then finished our game of dominoes with a bit less joking and touching than usual.

He caught me up fast. He was now a lifeguard, and since they didn't have lifeguarding chairs, walking up and down the beach was the entirety of his job. We stepped around a couple of boys throwing sand in each other's faces, no one to tell them to stop. Rogelio wouldn't say why he left the school, but it seemed that a story existed. "You must miss the kids," I said. He only shook his head and grinned. He seemed amused by himself.

He never said anything about my head—maybe it was no longer bleeding—so I said nothing about his diminishing body. We hopped on his motorcycle. I guess his shift had ended.

"Hold on tight," he reminded me.

I sat behind him, his rear and my crotch vying for the same space, my big white knees bumping into his bony, brown thighs. "Pinche gringo," he laughed, reaching back to squeeze my leg. "Pinche Richard."

When we passed the harbor I looked to see if I could spot a particular sailboat. I had met a couple of middle-aged men from Vermont that summer, an owner of a concession stand company and a woodworker who got what he thought was a great deal on a beat-up sixty-foot schooner built in South Africa. They planned to sail to Panama and back, a route the business owner had sailed in his twenties, but he hadn't set foot on a boat since. The woodworker's daughter dropped out of college to join the crew, and the business owner met an itinerant Australian woman at a bar who also joined. The men had big plans to raise the deck, redo the cabin floors, and update the bathrooms. The boat was quite old and decrepit, perhaps better suited for day trips or a maritime museum. I didn't see the old schooner as we passed the harbor. I wondered if they were lost at sea, if they had returned to their previous lives, if they ended up on different boats with different people.

We did an entire loop of the island the way we used to late at night when the roads were empty. We'd go over a speed bump and I'd say, "Topo," and he'd laugh a little then say, "Topito" because it was a small bump, though it seemed average sized to me, but Rogelio liked to add "ito" to every word, perhaps to keep what life contained small and innocent. We could hear the ocean crashing against the rocks, but we could only see the road ahead and blackness below. We'd trade beautiful and ugly stories about our families. I told him how as a teenager my dad wrote my mom love notes on orange peels and how after four decades they'd still rather be with each other than be alone or with someone young and new. He told me how on Saturday afternoons his entire family of aunts and uncles and cousins gathered for dominoes and ceviche. I told him how in her eighties my great aunt was assaulted by an eighteen-year-old in a CVS parking lot. I was newly a teenager when it happened and couldn't figure out how any young man could want sex from anyone but a young woman. Rogelio told me how he lost an uncle at sea and a brother in a motorcycle accident. He then accelerated hard and my helmet fell to the back of my neck. I scooted into him and pressed my inner thighs into his outer thighs.

Now it was daytime and taxis and tourists on golf carts cluttered the road even at the southern tip, which used to be wild and jungle-like but now sprouting up were modern houses in the shapes of seashells and lighthouses.

That summer, I had left the island in a hurry. We were on a field trip to the beach, and Patricia—one of my students, eight years my junior, a well-built child who was already proficient in teasing men through both words and body language—and I were clinging to the same inflatable raft, letting the rhythm of the gentle waves nearly lull us to sleep. Our legs must have brushed a couple of times before we let them fully tangle. Nothing else happened, just legs twisted around legs, an evasion of eye contact, a little nervous laughter, and then we released. In class I found myself giving her too much attention or completely ignoring her, not knowing what it was I wanted out of her, but knowing I wanted something, even if it was just confirmation that I existed and she existed, and that she hadn't yet worried what any of that meant. I left a note for Rogelio and the school claiming family troubles at home, though my family was splendid—no money or health problems, no substance abuse, no major rifts, only a normal amount of anxiety and depression.

We'd almost completed a full loop of the island when a small blond-headed figure with the posture and confidence of a self-assured adult appeared in the middle of the road. Rogelio honked and pretended to swerve into her as we passed, but the girl remained unfazed.

"Turn around," I demanded.

"See something you like?"

"You never stop, do you?" I said.

"We'll take her back to my place and feed her."

"She doesn't look hungry."

"She looks hungry."

We flipped around and pulled up even to the girl who was strutting down the middle of the road. She was still only in her bathing suit. I hopped off the bike, and she pretended not to notice me.

"What are you doing out here?" I said.

She squinted at me, perhaps because of the sun, but pretended not to recognize me.

"We'll give you a ride back to the beach," I said.

I took off my helmet and she stopped squinting, shot me a look of recognition, then tried to look at the top of my head, and said, "It looks better. Hey, have you seen my dad?"

"He's probably at the bar. He's just trying to enjoy vacation before going back to work."

Rogelio parked his bike on the side of the road and joined us. Taxis and golf carts zipped by, some honking and swerving way out of the way, others nearly clipping us.

"Let's go to my place and regroup," Rogelio said. "The road is dangerous." He pinched my arm and then moved closer to the girl.

"He took off with that guy," the girl said. "I tried to follow them, but they started running."

"He'll be back at the hotel tonight. Tomorrow at the latest," I said. But the girl looked at me incredulously.

The girl's thin and toned body was not unlike mine or Rogelio's. I imagined what it'd be like if we all hugged, pressed ourselves into each other, our hip bones clanking in this awkward triangular formation, but she didn't need such a thing from us.

•

On Rogelio's bike the girl sat between us. It was the only way to ensure she wouldn't fall off. I tried to keep her in, but I also tried to keep from making even the slightest movement. Rogelio reached back and patted the girl's calf, "Smooth," he said.

We blazed through an isolated section of the upper road across from the navy airstrip where Americans built houses, where men in uniform gave a red helicopter a daily sponge bath, where the island was only a quarter mile wide. The Americans brought in enough hot water and Internet to feel just close enough and just far enough from what was and still might be home. They now owned quite a bit of the island. It was easy to want more than one home, to have somewhere to live without all of your decisions.

On the beach we all fell asleep, or at least I did. I woke to the girl giggling, rolling in and out of Rogelio's tickling hands, and telling him to "stop it" in a playful tone that most men would translate to mean *keep going*. We were in the same spot as earlier in the day. In an hour or so the sun would set. Families were leaving the beach to wash up for dinner. Couples in street clothes and glazy-eyed individuals emerged in anticipation of an orange-and-pink horizon. "If no one shows up before dark, we'll try to find your hotel," I muttered to the girl, only one eye open.

I tried hard to stay awake, but the sand was the softest most forgiving surface I'd lain upon in weeks. Every so often I extended my leg to touch the girl's leg just to make sure she was still there. I kept telling myself five more minutes, but eventually I gave in to my exhaustion.

When I woke, the girl's head was tucked into my armpit, my arm wrapped around her shoulder. I sprang up and looked around, but the only light came from a scattering of stars and a sliver of moon. The darkness was a relief. Down by the water where the girl's dad and brother had played catch, two small figures folded into each other moved gently with the rhythm of the waves. I wondered what would be the appropriate way to wake the girl. If she were my child I might touch her shoulder and use the word *honey*. She slept so deeply though, a gentle touch might only comfort her. I knelt down, my hands hovering over her. Uncontrolled by my brain they moved spastically through the air in erratic patterns like a raver on a good trip. Again, I found myself in a bad spot—I'd be a strange man returning a girl in a bikini after dark to her mother. Or I'd have to abandon her, take her to my hotel room, or wake up at her side. I considered a life on the island with the girl. I'd open a medical clinic and enroll her in the school. We'd only have each other to answer to. Without her family the girl would avoid great pain and disappointment. I would never replace her dad, but I would never leave her. I would write to my life-partner-to-be and let her know she was right that I had always been looking to disconnect from those who knew me best, that I indeed felt more at home among strangers. I'd fit right in around these parts. I pulled my hands back, popped up, and shuffled towards the water. The two people wrapped up in each other's limbs were teenagers. The boy gave me a nod, but I couldn't return the gesture. I probably scowled. I was embarrassed for both of us, for anyone who had ever made love, anyone who had ever desired another. I went back to the girl, knelt at her side and peeled her arm off the sand. I ran my fingers up and down it looking for bumps or bruises, any sign of Rogelio. I put her arm down then ran the back of my hand from her neck, over her ribs, stomach, and skipped down to her leg. If I found anything suspect I would go to Rogelio and teach him a lesson. But who was I to say what was suspect and what lesson could I teach? The duo down by the water untangled and settled onto their backs. The boy put his arm around the girl and pointed to the sky, probably telling her, *your eyes are as bright as the moon.* I lay down at the girl's side and let my hand rest on her bony shoulder. She rolled onto her side so that she was facing me and her eyes flicked open. "It's still you," she said. Somehow those few words made me feel empty, used, abandoned. I had already decided I was an important person in this little person's life. But I was just a stranger and tomorrow we would find her family and all of our lives would fall back into place. Though tonight—tonight I would stay awake and make sure no one lay a finger on her, and I would rub her back so she didn't dream of loneliness or abandonment or wandering hands in unwanted places. "Yep, it's just me," I whispered.

A Normal Walk

Until we sipped it down, the coffee sloshed out of our mugs and onto the sleeves of our fall jackets. It was just a walk; a normal walk around the neighborhood. I led the way. I turned down the newer, sunny streets with sidewalks and young couples with small children, and avoided those with old maples holding onto their browning leaves. The mid-November air quickly chilled the coffee even though it wasn't what mid-November air used to be. We drank the coffee, happily. Happy to have mouths that drank. Legs that walked. Hands that held things. The sun warmed our backs and necks. It radiated through our cores and out our limbs. It tickled our brains in a way that made us want to comment on whatever was in front of us: a nicely landscaped lawn, a low front tire, a toddler helping her dad push her baby sister's stroller. We were happy to have so much in front of us.

As usual we made our way to the pond. We had learned to find it beautiful even though twenty years ago this same man-dug ditch filled with piped-in water had us longing for either rural or urban surroundings; somewhere with natural bodies of water or ones every bit intended to look manmade. For years the suburban in-between had us unnerved, unsettled, anxiously looking around for escape routes. A pair of wading ducks took off into the air once we got too close. He was amazed, he claimed he'd never seen ducks fly. Not once in his fifty-one years. But we had seen ducks fly just last week. And he'd grown up on a farm surrounded by ponds.

"They're great fliers," I said. "They could cross an ocean."

"You know what?" he said. "This pond would be perfect for ice-skating."

I told him I'd never ice-skated on a pond and he said he used to do it all the time as a pudgy teenager until the time he slipped and hit his head and was raced to the emergency room fifteen miles down the road. Of course I'd heard that story eight or ten or twelve or twenty-three times, but he'd also already heard me say I've never iced-skated on a pond nine or thirteen or twenty-two times. It was normal: a couple batting back and forth the same stories over several decades, each repeat telling sandwiched between new and unrepeatable moments.

We kept on, putting one foot in front of the other, our non-coffee drinking arms loose and free at our sides, a gentle breeze breaking across our faces. Everything felt good. We passed other walkers. One woman had a giant dog. Neither of us knew what kind it was, but he said he liked very small dogs and I said I liked very big dogs. Of course we already knew this about each other. We were finally planning to replace Felix who was our black Lab, the only pet we ever had as a family, his legacy becoming grander by the day. We'd visited the rescue shelter three times now, each time quickly pulled towards different breeds. "Maybe you should get two," the teenaged-girl volunteer suggested on our most recent trip with an earnestness that was slightly more refreshing than irritating.

At the top of the hill, once we recovered our breaths, he said, "I talked to Hannah this morning, I'm worried about her."

We had almost named our daughter Hannah, but once we spent a few moments with her, once we heard her cry and felt the warmth of her tiny grip, and saw the way she looked at us, we agreed her name should be Elise. Hannahs sprang into the world ready to take on whatever came their way with temerity. Elises were apprehensive and deliberate and sensitive. Sometimes he called her Jake, our son's name, but he had been doing that since they were young, and he always caught himself.

"Oh?" I said.

"She doesn't sound like herself."

"Who?" I said. My mind had wandered to Jake's girlfriend. They had visited last weekend, and though she tried hard, complimenting our wild garden and herbaceous cooking and the cheerful color of our bathroom walls, there was something she said that lingered. Her parents, she said, had been high school sweethearts, but they were still happy together. The *still* troubled me; it was even obvious to a skinny, eye shadow-wearing nineteen-year-old—who would be one of many girlfriends we would meet—that partners living happily together over multiple decades defied all odds. Or maybe it simply embarrassed her that her parents never had certain kinds of experiences.

"Elise," he said, impatiently. "School's too much these days. How can you take six classes and expect to have any fun? The brain can't work under that kind of pressure. She has no confidence. She's not sniffing out her true passion. She still wants to be pre-med. The brain can't work!"

"She'll find her passion," I said, "And if she doesn't, she'll still have a good life. We made out okay."

We didn't worry about Jake. He got worse grades than Elise, but he always managed to meet the right people and follow his interests, which as far as we could tell were money and people. He landed summer internships and was always getting invited on vacations with his friends' families. But Elise was very serious. She needed to feel she had a purpose bigger than her own fulfillment. When she was a little girl, she said she wanted to be a teacher because it was important that children learned so they could know things. As a teenager she wanted to be a journalist because the truth mattered more than anything. And now she wanted to be a doctor because she did well in high school biology and how else would she pay back college loans, and she would like people to depend on her—I could remember once having a similar desire.

There were three turns to get home. A right, then a left, then another left. I led the way. I was always a half step ahead. I'd finished my coffee and dangled the mug at my waist, only my pointer finger wrapped around the handle. He continued to sip from his mug and wipe his mouth on his wrist. We passed by a man in his thirties scooping up leaves with a Frisbee while a Scottish Terrier sprinted circles around the yard. We exchanged hellos. Everyone said hello in our neighborhood, but conversation rarely went further unless you had your dog with you.

"Now that's a nice dog," he said, once we were out of earshot of the Terrier's owner. "Reminds me of Felix."

"We're done with Felix, we need a dog who will surprise us."

"Surprise us," he repeated, "then maybe we should get a Macaw like our friend down by the bike path."

"Are you kidding? We'd have to get two, and write them into our wills, and do you really want your pets talking to you?"

"I guess it depends. We could get a whole new perspective on what's going on in our lives," he laughed a little.

"I'm glad you're always you," I said, smiling.

"I'll never be anyone else," he said. "That much I can promise."

It was said both jokingly and seriously that I was robbing the cradle, the three years between us were big back then. My mother feared his eye would wander to younger women earlier than expected, she never said this explicitly, but it's not hard for a daughter to read between the lines. The same way Elise complained that she knew I had a hard time imagining her in the exam room, even though I always told her I thought she'd make a great neurologist or cardiologist if that was what she wanted to do. Now here we were, thirty years later, happy enough in the suburbs, two young-adult children. Our child rearing near finished. Roles would begin to reverse sooner than later. And he, my beloved husband, was calling our daughter by the wrong name. It was funny how one day you had a plan that you were so serious about and then before you knew it decades had passed and you realized how silly it was to have a plan, to try to control anything, and now you were happy to go for walks and talk to your kids on the phone, but there was still something in you that wanted to reach forward for an old plan, and when you thought about it, it became a desperate kind of reach because what you had left in front of you could only get smaller, so you said to your husband—in your front yard while brushing up against your dried up peony stalks, before the walk was over because once you were inside you would retreat to your office and he would go to his reading chair, a house you loved and never wanted to leave, but the idea of dying in it made you all kinds of disappointed—"Let's get the hell out of here." He'd heard you say this many times before, but always unconvincingly, ready to argue against yourself, the emphasis on *hell*, but this time he heard the emphasis on *out* and he noted your eyes were not squinting playfully, or maybe he looked at your empty mug and saw one last drop of coffee at the brim and decided it was a sign. "Before it's too late," he said, trying his best to make it sound more like a question than a declaration.

In the Family

Always you waited until the hottest part of the day to mow the lawn. You never let it grow more than an inch. Sometimes Randall and I caught you picking wedgies from your shorts, which split up the side of your thigh, revealing where your leg hair tapered off. From across the yard, you looked like my dad: tall, pale and not terribly out of shape. Randall's dad was even taller. So Randall said.

Now that I'm a man, now that I work long hours during the summer instead of playing endless games of Wiffle Ball, now that I live a couple of hours away, now that your shorts don't strike me as being so short, now that you hire the Thomure boy from across the street to mow your lawn, I feel I owe you an apology.

If Randall were around, he would disagree. He'd claim you were a grown man and knew what you were doing. You even had a boy of your own, so my dad said, and he must have been quite ashamed of you. So Randall said. Your son was so ashamed that he dropped out of school and said yes to drugs and hung around the ratty part of town between the laundromat and the convenience store, a dented-up bike between his legs and a cigarette in his mouth until eventually he disappeared.

You were ashamed of him because he didn't look enough like you. Too ashamed to let him inside your house to rest and hydrate. *Shoo shoo, get get*, as if he were a stray, rabid cat. You hung him out to dry. But he's lucky he got away. So Randall said. Just imagine what goes on in there. You even had a wife somewhere, so my dad said, perhaps somewhere in that house of yours, but we had no way of knowing. Randall said your boy didn't look like your wife either, and so something had to give. All we really knew was what we saw, which was you mowing the lawn, sometimes straight across and sometimes diagonally, sweat rolling down your bare back and collecting at the waist. On occasion, one of us would slug a Wiffle Ball into your yard. You would let the mower idle, bend over holding up your shorts, and pick up the ball and throw it back, a few fresh clippings attached. Always I was impressed by the strength of your arm, and Randall would say his dad could throw twice as far. You said nothing because the mower was too loud, but you never seemed annoyed. Randall joked that you liked picking up our balls, which only then seemed hilarious.

My dad is not my real dad, but I like him enough. I think I would like him less if he had played some role in making me. As is, it's easy to enjoy his crooked nose and frizzy hair, the way he always gives a little wave when he says hello to someone, even when it's over the phone, how he chews on chicken bones after all the meat is gone.

Randall used to talk about his dad so much, there were no questions left to ask. I guess that was the point. I never went to Randall's house. I never met his dad. My house was closer to school and had a larger yard. At our baseball games, Randall's mom made herself small on the top row of the bleachers, her arms crisscrossed over her chest. When we were in ninth grade, Randall had a baby sister. Randall called her "the baby" but rarely mentioned her once she was born. I never saw her close up, never got to see if she had Randall's big forehead or fat lower lip or sharp chin, features that I had, too, and were common in kids at our school.

When I visit my dad I look for you in your yard, even in the winter, but you're never there. This time it's summer, muggier and stickier than I ever remember. I ask my dad if you still live here and he looks surprised and says, "Of course. Where would he go?" I say, "I guess I don't know. Sometimes people leave." Then my dad says how you're still a young man, only a couple of years older than himself. I nod, I guess in agreement. Even though my dad seems older than he used to, it doesn't bother me. We've already had a good run, though of course I'd be devastated if it ended. With my mom, it ended too early for me to be devastated. For that, I'm grateful.

Before driving back, I tell my dad I've met a woman that I'd like him to meet. "She's a Capricorn," I say jokingly because I know what my dad really wants to know. "And she's not from around these parts."

He would like me to be more specific. His look says, *Define "these parts."*

"She's Canadian."

My dad tries his best to look excited instead of relieved. He likes to say how we should diversify our family. The alternative could be dangerous. But when I ask what exactly he means, he just says something like, "I want you to be happy and healthy," which always comes out genuinely but is starting to wear on me. He might as well just go ahead and say it. In my senior year, our high school printed a pamphlet titled "Know Your Partner Before You Know Your Partner." They were handed out in class, posted to walls, and mailed to our homes. The pamphlet was full of vague language and typos, and included a five-step guide to knowing your partner. Step four was *Ask lots of questions about you're partner's family* and step five was *Meat your partner's family and make sure you're an appropriate amount compatible.* The pamphlet was followed by a letter from the Superintendent. He apologized for the typos, but they were in a hurry and simply getting the message out was his top priority.

"She must hate the heat then," my dad says.

"I don't know. She's really not much of a complainer," I say.

"Sounds like a good catch."

I'm backing out of the driveway, all packed up, already gave my dad a big hug, when I finally see you in your front yard. You're lying on your back on an orange-and-purple towel. You're naked. All that hair you used to keep all over your body is nowhere to be seen. If only Randall were here! I put the car in park and saunter onto your property. You know someone is coming because my figure messes with your sun. Once I get closer, I can see you're in a skimpy tan bathing suit, nearly the color of your skin. I come within a towel's length of you, and then you sit up. You flip up your sunglasses, and I can see your eyes have sunk further back into your head.

"The Lazarus boy," you say. I can tell you really want to remember my name but not necessarily so you can use it. As more of a memory test. "How's your pops?"

"I'm sorry," I say, but it comes out more like a question, as though I was asking you to repeat yourself.

"He's a good guy," you say, as if this isn't a given.

I feel awkward standing over you, which must be obvious because you pop up and invite me in for lemonade. I'm silent too long to say, "No thanks, I better be on my way," so I follow you inside.

"It's pretty much just me here these days," you say, then leave me in your living room.

While you're in the kitchen cracking ice out of a plastic tray, I move around lightly on your dull pink carpet. There is a fireplace, a couch, a coffee table and a pair of puffy blue chairs, one of which is occupied by a set of binoculars. Not a single photo. Binoculars though, this is too easy, Randall would have a field day!

You come in with two lemonades but catch me off guard— I must still be looking at the binoculars.

"Oh, those old things," you say.

I smile gently, which seems like a mistake. My dad is just next door, and I am younger and stronger than you, but who knows what else you have lying around here.

You hand me a glass of lemonade. "Let me ask, are you afraid of heights?"

I should say yes, but I can't look another human in the eye and lie, and the truth is, my dad and I have jumped out of airplanes together and I'm not sure you don't already know this. "Not at all," I say.

You hand me the binoculars and lead me upstairs and down a brief hallway with two shut doors on each side. I stop and take a good look at you. I'm surprised by the boniness of your upper back and the power of your hamstrings. You pull down a hatch from the ceiling, which folds

out into a ladder, and we climb up into an empty attic and then out a
window onto a section of flat roof. There is a leafy potted plant and
a half-full water bottle, two plastic chairs, and two plates with bread
crusts.

"Have a look."

I see my childhood bedroom window, big and blurry, then refocus
and I'm relieved that I can't see inside my room. I look down our street.
Nothing I've never seen before. A street that never turns, two-story
houses with rectangular yards split in half by walkways. A posse of
kids on bikes, all with similar haircuts and riding postures. An elderly
woman pulled along by a Golden Retriever.

You gesture for me to have a seat, but when I go to sit down you
tell me that's your seat and the other one is mine. "Go ahead and keep
looking if you'd like. I can look anytime," you say.

But I don't want to, so I put the binoculars on my lap. "What do
you look for? Anything in particular?"

You smile at me as if to say, *finally, we're going to have a conversation.* "Well, I'm retired now and it's pretty much just me here. You see
what I'm saying?"

I only nod.

"I guess I could join a club or call up some old friends, but with
folks my age I don't have much to show for. And I like it up here and you
never know, might see something of note. Something that could change
things. Beautiful or rotten."

"Or both," I add.

You look pleased with my contribution. "You know, if you ever need
space from your Pops, you can come on over. Anytime," you say.

Randall said you were into us. But you probably liked us because we
weren't your problem. You probably didn't even like us. You just didn't
mind us. But now you seem to actually like me because I'm an adult,
but not the kind you feel you have to prove something to.

"I live out of town," I say.

You give an ah-ha nod, as if you had forgotten who I am and just
now recalled a conversation with my dad, he standing on our driveway
in work clothes, you on the edge of your yard, shirtless and sweaty for
no good reason.

"But thank you," I say.

"And your baseball buddy?"

I must give you an empty look.

"He kind of looked like you actually. A good strong arm from what I saw."

"He also left town," I say, looking off to the west hoping the sun will sear my eyes. The truth is, Randall could be anywhere. He wouldn't say where he was going or if he'd come back.

I finish my lemonade then tell you I need to use the bathroom. You tell me twice how to get there, but I was never so good at remembering my lefts from rights.

The room you send me to on the second floor is not a bathroom. I push open the door and enter a bedroom with baby blue walls streaked with brushstrokes and a strip of white just before the wall becomes ceiling. The blinds are tightly shut and only let in the slightest ray of light. At the far side of the room, a wooden desk cluttered with textbooks. At the foot of the bed, a dresser with a half cup of water on top. The bed neatly made. Tucked neatly into the bed, a boy. Not a living, breathing boy—a wooden boy. Only his head and a little bit of neck showing. The sheets snug, revealing his trim physique. A fat lower lip and your drifty eyes; frustrated as if he's having trouble falling asleep or waiting for something and has no idea what or who it is, or how long it will be. If only Randall were here!

Working Backwards

My students ask me how long I've had my beard. I tell them I don't know because the truth is, I don't. "Greater than eight years, less than thirteen," I say. This seems accurate.

"Have you even trimmed it?" Jacob says. He wears plaid shorts and a snug T-shirt no matter the weather. A few weeks ago he was rocking a pencil thin mustache and a full head of hair. Today he comes in with stubble and a mohawk.

It's the beginning of class and we're waiting for the stragglers to lope in and make a bunch of noise turning desks sideways, squeezing into our asymmetrical circle, and then unzipping, unbuckling, unsnapping bags. I've given up on trying to scare/guilt/bribe them into punctuality.

"It's been a while, but yes," I say. "My best friend wanted me to shave for his wedding, so I compromised by trimming."

At this point in the semester I have no problem answering personal questions. We only have two sessions remaining after today, we've already made our impressions and proven or not proven ourselves, gained or not gained trust, and they've already filled out evaluations, so what's the worst that can happen?

I'm only a master's student. I never cared too much for school, was never very good at it; each semester my students are amused and pleasantly surprised when I divulge this, the few overachievers wondering how a former B-plus student will ever teach them anything. I don't tell them I left my first college mid-semester because I can't answer the question that always comes next.

"You should shave for our last class," Shay says. Unlike the others, Shay always looks directly at me, never offering the slightest facial cue. When she speaks, everyone shuts up and listens.

"I would but I'm afraid of what I might find," I joke, pulling a patch of hair under my chin, but no one laughs because it's not clear that I'm joking. My jokes are solid conceptually, but I need to work on my delivery. I don't intone the most effective syllable, I hold a straight face too long, or I rush the punch line. Every now and then I get lucky, or they give me a pity laugh.

"You'd probably look super young," Jacob says. "Like they-might-even-card-you young."

I still get carded sometimes, but it's clear that it's just a formality. I haven't had a bartender or liquor store clerk look at me suspiciously in at least five years. My beard is big and bushy and if you look closely you'll notice a small invasion of gray hairs. I get the feeling I look older than I actually am, which is okay with me knowing that if I shaved I'd look like any other thirty-one-year-old man. I have no reason to believe otherwise.

"Okay, I'll shave for the last class, but only if you all agree to wear something ridiculous that day."

"We agree!" Isto says, ripping open a bag of Lays. Isto transferred this semester from a community college in the northeast and often munches on chips and blurts out.

"Define ridiculous," Jacob says.

"Hmmm," I say, "how about something that makes you feel uncomfortable, awkward, unlike yourself." The idea feels a little Will-Schuester-*Glee*ish, which is disconcerting. I notice my sense of humor getting a little cheesier, a little more dad-like every semester.

"Like a wig!" Isto says.

"Anything," I say, "anything you otherwise wouldn't be caught dead in." I look around the circle and notice no one is touching their phone, slouching, or taking note of the scuffs on my brown scuffed-up shoes. Instead, their eyes are running up and down my face like a razor.

"We agree," Shay says, everyone else nodding.

I stand up and write on the board:

Friday: come to class dressed like a freak—*No nudity*

I go straight to Gutwein's office to gloat about my brilliant idea, to rub in his face how my students are responding to me, that they see me as more than a writing teacher. His desk is cluttered with stacks of books and piles of manuscripts. His walls covered in posters that say things like, "Yes, I did mean to offend you," and "WWYOJPD? (What would your old Jewish professor do?)." A pair of golf shoes dangle from a hook, a bag of clubs propped up on the floor beneath. He's reading an email on his computer, his back to me.

"What do you want, douchebag?" he says.

"What if I was one of your colleagues?"

"Then I would have called you a fucking douchebag."

"Seriously, how'd you know I wasn't someone important?"

He swivels his chair around so that he's facing me. His beard is bushy and gray, his hair is long in the back and over the ears and bald on top. I'm comforted by his nose, which is similar in size and shape to my dad's.

"Those assholes would send me an email. So what the fuck do you want?"

"We have a game tonight." I no longer want to talk about teaching.

"Oh yeah? I'll take the over on the thirty-point spread."

"I wouldn't," I say. "It's at nine, in case you're interested."

"That's snoozing time for me, but good luck, don't have a heart attack."

"Still on for Saturday lunch?"

"I told you, I'm taking you somewhere special where Jews really shouldn't go."

He grins and I feel my face flushing red.

•

I get back from my rec league basketball game and there she is, Isabel, my life partner, wrapped up in a wool blanket, sitting Indian style on the couch, reading something thick and theoretical. I'm drawn to her for intangible reasons I can't quite articulate; the way it feels to be in her presence, comfortable yet fraught and always with potential for a wheeze-inducing laugh.

"So," she says, glancing up from her book, "how was it?"

"You're not going to believe it, we won! Actually, we blew them out!" I inhale and give a dramatic pause to signal a joke is on its way. "By one point," I add.

Our team, the Moral Victories, has been in the league three years and until tonight had never won a game. We're the oldest and least athletic team. All but two of us have beards, all but one of us has a paunch, all of us have life partners, none of us played high school basketball. But tonight we used our maturity and life experience to slow down the pace (I mean REALLY slow it down: we averaged nearly a minute per possession) and lure a team of rowdy teenagers into a frenetic style of play, tossing up bad shots on offense and committing frequent reaching fouls on defense. With two minutes left, down by only one point, we went into stall mode and simply passed the ball around the perimeter, from wing to the top of the key to the other wing and back. Our young opponents pressured the ball with quick feet and active hands, careful not to foul. One of their players called out from the bench, "Just take it. They got no handle." But they were never able to steal the ball and with five seconds left, Truman, the only guy on our team who shoots over 30 percent, took one hard dribble towards the hoop then pulled up and kissed a rainbow jumper off the glass. You would have thought we had won a championship; we pulled Truman to the floor and piled on top of him, every one of us trying to slap a hand onto his sweaty flesh. When we untangled from our pile, breathing heavily, we lined up and shook hands with the stunned, sinewy youngsters. In the plastic bleachers, the three teenaged girls who witnessed our victory hunched over their phones.

Isabel finishes reading a sentence then looks up. "You're the sportsman of the year," she says, clicking out lead from her mechanical pencil and underlining a section in the middle of the page. My joke about a one-point blowout didn't land.

"And the headband?" she says.

I pull the soaking wet piece of cloth from my mane of frizzy brown hair and dangle it in front of her. "It worked great. Not only did it keep my bangs out of my eyes, but look how much sweat it absorbed."

"You are disgusting."

"I play hard."

"Go shower so we can go to the store. We're out of tee-pee and ice cream."

At the grocery store Isabel leads us to the ice cream section because she says she won't make it through her book without something sweet and fatty. It used to be midnight runs to Dunkin' Donuts but now she's trying to kick that habit. She says it's not good for an individual to run on Dunkin'. We're standing in front of a dozen brands of ice cream and a frozen fruit section labeled "toppings." She pulls open a glass door and a blast of cold slaps me in the face.

"Bell, my dad is pestering me for a date," I say.

"How about December 21, 2012," Isabel says, studying the ingredients of the Edy's Cookie Dough.

"That's in two years, and isn't it the day the Mayans predict the world to end?"

"It can be an end-of-the-world-themed wedding."

"Weddings already have a built-in theme, they're wedding-themed."

"What is maltodextrin?" Isabel says, rotating the carton of ice cream in her palms.

"And if the Mayans are right?"

"We won't have to stress over the money we spent on photography and linens." She shakes her head at the ingredient list and returns the ice cream to the freezer then shuffles over to the frozen fruit. "I can't believe they're calling fruit, *toppings*. Only in the Midwest."

"I can think of worse things to call it."

"That's not the point."

She shuffles back to the Edy's, pulls out the Cookie Dough and tosses it into the cart.

"We don't have to call it a wedding, you know. We could call it something like a Romantic Alliance Celebration."

"Louie, my sports star, we have plenty of time. We're young enough and the world isn't just going to explode."

"But we don't know for sure who will be around next year or the year after."

My dad assures me my mom is okay, that she's not going anywhere anytime soon, but his eagerness about our wedding date is disconcerting. Usually he's the last person in the room to assert an opinion, to make a special request on his behalf—he's never once sent back food at a restaurant.

"Okay, tell me the truth about why you ditched out of your first college and then we'll sit down with a calendar."

"I've told you, I can't remember the details. It was forever ago."

"Why don't you remember anything from your childhood? We don't even know who you are!"

"I told you about our family vacation to Wyoming and the souvenir shop owner who asked my dad if it's true that Jews believe in unicorns."

"You have like three stories. Anyway, how do I know you didn't beat up a dog? Marriage is supposed to be forever and I don't want to be stuck with a guy who goes around kicking the crap out of dogs."

"By now I would have already beaten up our neighbor's dog with all his barking."

"You've punched the wall."

"You have too."

Isabel sighs as she always does when I deny her my parting-ways-with-my-first-college story. But the truth is, the details have been long repressed. I spent the first year after leaving college at my parents' house. I slept in my older brother's childhood room and worked as a bagger at Kroger. Each time a parent of an old high school classmate slid their groceries down the moving rubber belt, I became more and more convinced by my public narrative that I was taking time off school to mature, so I could figure out the classes I *really* wanted to take, and therefore wouldn't waste my parents' hard-earned money. The classmates' parents would nod and say something like, *Maybe Sarah should do the same,* or, *You'll figure things out,* or *Hmmmm.*

"This is a disgrace," Isabel says, gazing down another frozen food aisle. "Now they're calling pie *fruit.*"

"Better than calling it *crust.*"

"I guess it would be too obvious to call it *pie.*"

"How about this, I'll go to a hypnotist during break."

"Now you're talking!"

"I'm serious."

"I am too. I've never been more serious."

"But you have to promise not to leave me."

"You know I'll never make that promise." Isabel snatches my nose like I'm a child, then skips off and disappears down the toilet paper aisle.

"Fifty is kind of young to have a stroke," Isto says.

It's our second to last class and we're discussing Stephanie's essay about her dad. Stephanie plays on the volleyball team, always turns in work days before it's due and comes to office hours every week with dozens of questions that she starts to answer before I can even open my mouth. She was worried she wouldn't be able to hold it together in class and I was worried I wouldn't respond appropriately to any insensitive comments or that my eyes wouldn't soften.

"Aubrey Plaza had a stroke," Jacob says, smugly.

Everyone looks at Isto and nods. Stephanie has her hands cupped over her mouth. It takes a second for the name Aubrey Plaza to mean something to me, most of their pop culture references go over my head, but this is a name I know. An image of *Parks and Recreation* descends upon me followed by a memory of a recent dream, and then I let a shrill laugh escape. Olivia and Jacob and a few others give me a you-are-the-weirdest-instructor-we've-ever-had look.

"Actually, Aubrey Plaza was in my dream the other night," I say. When I told Isabel about the dream, we were on the couch reading and I used the name April because I couldn't remember her name in real life. "Somebody has a new celebrity crush," Isabel said, smiling and poking me in the ribs.

Isto makes a middle school-like "Ooooooh" and a few others laugh.

"It wasn't like that," I'm quick to say.

"She's pretty cute. I would hit it," Jacob says.

"No, no," I say, "it was in a grocery store."

"Right on!" Isto blurts out.

"Kinky," Jacob says.

"No, no. She was just giving out samples of Luna Bars."

"Kinky," Isto says, looking to Jacob for approval.

"Lunas are for women," Olivia says, shaking her head in disgust. Olivia's round face is always caked in makeup and she usually wears sweatpants, but today she's in a suit, something about a career fair. She rarely talks but frequently shakes her head, firmly disagreeing with whatever is being said.

A few snickers and side comments, my face becomes warm and tingly, and then we go back to Stephanie's essay. Almost everyone agrees that Stephanie should spend more time developing scenes with her dad when he was well so that the reader knows him as more than a voiceless man in a stark white room. Stephanie nods, her mouth clamped shut, respecting the author gag rule.

We finish discussing Stephanie's essay and we still have seven minutes left, but I have nothing else prepared. When I dismiss class early I feel like I'm letting my students down, not giving them their money's worth, even though they dart out of the room like they're running from a fire. Today though, they seem less eager to race off to the bar, gym, library, frat house, wherever it is they go. They're staring at me and I'm staring back.

"I saw you at Fresh Market last night," Shay says, taking over the room. "Who was the girl?"

"I didn't see you."

"I kept my distance, looked like you were arguing."

"So who was she?" Jacob says.

"She's my life partner."

"Your wife?" Isto says.

"Not yet, but we're life partners. For life."

"Better put a ring on it," Olivia says.

"She's pretty. Sort of has an Alison Brie thing going," Shay says.

"Thanks," I say, but my mind is blanking on the name Alison Brie. I toggle between Isabel, Aubrey Plaza, and an old photo of my mom in her wedding dress. I think how Isabel is the only person I've ever met who I would want to spend hours with every day. "She's working on her PhD," I say, hoping I don't sound too proud or too annoyed.

When the bell rings, everyone is already shoving notebooks and pens into backpacks. I blurt out, "See you Friday. And don't be afraid to fly your freak flag high." Isto and Stephanie nod. They're always slow to pack up their things. Isto shakes the crumbs off his shirt, throws his foot onto his desk and ties his shoe, then looks at me and says, "Chipotle time!" Stephanie comes over and stands in front of me.

"I know you'll send me your comments and all that, but I just wanna ask now so I can get started on some changes tonight, do you agree that too much of the essay is in the hospital? I'm worried the reader might feel claustrophobic, like the walls of the hospital are caving in on them while reading, but that's how I actually feel when I visit him. But the walls aren't just physical walls, you know what I mean?"

"The hospital scenes are tense," I say, not knowing what advice to give. Not able to tell her I envy her situation, at least she knows what's going on. "Honestly, it made me very sad. I can only imagine. I'm imagining myself in your shoes and I'm very sad."

For the first time Stephanie has nothing to say. Eyes downcast, she nods, and I pull on my beard.

"I know it sounds bad," she finally says, looking up, "but I wanted everyone to feel sad."

"It doesn't sound bad," I say, but it comes off as a perfunctory line that one uses when not wanting to invite further conversation.

Gutwein's door is closed, but I can tell the light is on. I want to ask him if he's heard of Alison Brie, I want to find out how he would respond to Stephanie's essay, if he would have offered something more than feedback on the writing. I notice a new sign on his door that says: *Leave money and go away.* I knock, expecting to hear him shout out, "Come back never!" No response.

I don't feel like going home. I gaze down the dark hallway of closed doors. I suddenly feel nostalgia for working in an office. I miss being greeted by a receptionist and saying hello to the same people every day, talking about traffic and weather and hearing about the funny things that children do. These conversations feel warm and civil, and any kind of response works just fine.

I knock again. I put my ear to the door. It's quiet. I start to imagine the worst. Last semester he had his second heart attack during a department meeting while arguing with his nemesis about the shift in the required reading for undergrad majors in effort to better reach an increasingly diverse student body. I start to count. At twenty-two Mississippi I hear heavy breathing, and at thirty-one Mississippi it has evolved into full-blown snoring. Relieved, I open my wallet and find a crinkled, half-torn 20-peso bill that I've been carrying around for years. I write *do us all a favor and move south* on the bill and slide it under the door.

Isabel needs a break from reading, so she decides to go to her first Moral Victories game, though she still brings a book. She and a young woman with a baby are the only fans. In the first half I steal the ball out around the three-point line and have an easy fast break. A few steps before the hoop I turn my head to share a look with Isabel, perhaps give her a wink, but her gaze is down in her book. I take a hard dribble and jump as high as I've ever jumped. While in the air, one of my teammates shouts out, "Dunk it!" I lay it slightly too high off the backboard, and the ball rolls off the rim. Their point guard grabs the rebound and pushes it up the court. Isabel shouts from the bleachers, "Here we go Morals!"

In the second half I'm at the free throw line. I hit the first one, nothing but net and a teensy weensy bit of rim. Before my second free throw, during my four dribble, two backspin routine, number thirty-three on the Conquistadors, their cross-eyed center, mutters, "She's gonna miss. She's gonna miss." I shoot an ugly arcless shot and the ball clanks off the front of the rim. Number thirty-three grabs the board. Back on defense I strip the ball from him and we both end up on the ground going after it. He's under me, my thigh in his crotch, the ball locked in our four arms.

"Get off of me, you fag," he says, soft enough that only I hear it.

I roll away leaving the ball in his grip. I stand over him and say, "Don't you have a gay friend?"

He lifts himself up and says, "Only you," nudging me in the chest. I shove him back.

We both get teed up and ejected from the game. I sit silently on the bench, watching the Conquistadors slowly pull away. Number thirty-three pacing the sidelines, clapping and shouting out things like, "Let 'em shoot," and "Take it easy on these ladies."

On the way home Isabel says, "So, what was that?"

I only sigh and shake my head and ease my foot off the pedal to show that I can exercise control.

"You looked pretty angry. "

"It's a physical game," I say. I don't mention that it's my third technical foul of the season.

"Sometimes you get so angry."

"It was a loose ball, so I went for it. It's part of the game."

"You also shoved him."

"He's a bigot."

"So what? There are millions of bigots. I wish you'd take things less personally, let things roll off you, take yourself less seriously."

"Okay," I say, exhaling, "you're right." Cars swerve around us as we creep along at ten under the limit.

"I believe you're a good person, but sometimes you just keep things in too long."

"You're right. I'll start being more open from now on. I really will." But this is what I always say.

My bladder wakes me up early. I don't want to get out of bed. I lay on my back holding the comforter over my nose. Other than a streak of light sneaking through the blinds, our bedroom is dark and cozy. A mousy kissing sound escapes from Isabel's lips, but she is sound asleep and probably not dreaming of kissing, it's just a noise her mouth makes when she sleeps on her stomach. The first time I heard the sound I let my small jealous streak get the best of me, and I tapped her awake and demanded she tell me what she'd been dreaming of. She had no idea what I was getting at and told me never to wake her again unless there's a fire or I have a box of donuts. I hold my breath and push lightly off the mattress. Our bed is old and creaky, and Isabel requests that I no longer pole vault out of it.

In the bathroom mirror I see my mom, olive skin, chin-length salt and pepper hair, thick eyebrows and round cheeks. Eyes that reveal. I touch my face and am surprised to feel a mat of coarse hair. I blink myself fully awake and then there I am in the mirror. First I use scissors. The long curly hairs fall slowly like feathers. Then I coat my cheeks in soap and imagine I'm operating a plow on a snow-covered road.

"Looks good!" Isto says.

"How'd you do it?" Jacob says. "Electronic or manual?"

"Manual."

"That's rough," Isto says.

Jacob shoots him an annoyed look that says, *What do you know, kid? You can barely grow peach fuzz.*

I scan the room and notice the only person wearing something unusual is Olivia in a cowboy hat and red bandana floating over her chest. I look again trying to make something out of Isto's socks with flip-flops, Jacob's teal V neck T-shirt, Shay's French braid, but I've seen it all before.

"So you guys tricked me pretty good," I say.

They look at me like they're anticipating a punch line.

"You're just in your normal clothes." I try to sound lighthearted but it comes out bitter and annoyed.

"We didn't think you were serious," Stephanie says, she seems concerned.

"We forgot," Jacob says, "but personally, I would never shave for a bunch of hungover college kids."

"Is this gonna affect our grades?" Olivia says.

"Girl, you dressed up," Shay says.

Olivia tilts her cowboy hat and tightens her bandana. "O-M-G, I did."

"Yeah right," Jacob says, shaking his head. "It's called rush. It's called the Kappa barn dance. It's called lucky timing."

"She's a cowgirl," Isto says. "Pretty cool idea."

"We're sorry," Stephanie says.

The others, the few silent ones, look down at their shoes.

"Let's just forget about it," I say, rubbing my bare chin, trying to sound upbeat. "It's really no big deal."

"So, what was the point of this class?" I say. "I mean, in addition to credit and learning to write better, what's the point?"

"Come on, man, it's like the last day," Jacob says.

"It *is* the last day," Shay corrects him.

I stand up and they must see someone filled with rage because even Shay—who I imagine fears no one, not even an armed burglar—looks down at her shoes. Stephanie is the only one to hold her gaze, her eyes revealing that she knew I was pushing down something explosive all semester and she had been waiting for this moment, that she, too, had recently had this moment.

"Guys, I'm not joking," I say, my tone is sharp. I fantasize flipping over a desk or throwing it Bobby Knight style. I feel my hands tightening around the table's edge, my veins popping out.

"Hey, what's that thing on your chin?" Isto says.

"Yeah, man. You totally have some mark on your chin," Jacob says. "It's not a tat, is it?"

"It's kind of cool," Isto says. "Looks like a shadow of a butterfly."

"Not at all," Olivia says. "You should get that looked at."

I rub my chin and don't feel anything but smooth, soft skin. My frustration with my students has flattened and now spiking up is that nervous anticipatory feeling I get before the first class of the semester, waiting to see who walks through the door.

"Let's take a ten-minute break and you can go back to your places and put on something weird. You know, hold up your end of the deal."

"I live like twenty minutes from here," Jacob says.

"Seriously? You want us to go out in this cold?" Shay says.

"Ok, fine. Five-minute break. Stay in the building. I just want to go look at this chin thing."

"It's really not that bad," Stephanie says.

I pass the nearest bathroom and go to the one-person men's room tucked away near a cluster of oddly shaped adjuncts' offices. I prefer to avoid my students just before or just after one or both of us have moved our bowels. The mirror is too low so I bend my knees and tilt my head back. It's about the size of a quarter, but it's not round. It's a faint redish-brown with purple edges. Not a butterfly, more like a tulip. Now it has the slightest texture, like a sticker. I rub it, scratch it, rinse it with warm water, try to peel it off.

I walk the opposite direction from my classroom. Gutwein's door is ajar, so I knock and enter in one motion before he can say, "What the fuck do you want?" He's reading a manuscript, though seems to be thinking more than reading, his enormous head in his enormous hands. A tuft of gray hair sprouts out of his collar like a bouquet of weeds. I'm tilting my head back so he can see under my chin.

"What happened there?" he says.

"I'm not sure."

"I should have known you'd be even uglier under that hairy mask. As much as I hate helping you, I can recommend a great skin doctor, she's even a member of our tribe."

"Thanks, but I have a feeling it's nothing harmful. I have a vague memory of this thing, but I'm all blocked up. Wanna help me recall it?" I say, jokingly, but Gutwein is in one of his rare serious moods.

"Sure," he says. "Close your eyes. Don't worry, I'm not a priest."

It feels good to close my eyes.

"Now what do you remember about that disgusting mess on your chin?"

"I only remember a feeling."

"Guilt?"

"Shame."

"Let's try working backwards, I learned this from my therapist. We were addressing how I'm always checking up on Julia and how this pushes her away to the point that she only answers my calls if she's having car problems. Did you know I worked in a garage for seven years?"

"I've seen your calluses."

"Anyway, I insisted I was just your run-of-the-mill neurotic Jewish dad and there was no past event making me over-protective and I really just needed to change my personality and meet Julia somewhere in the middle. My therapist nodded along like that may very well be true, but then he had me work backwards from that very morning when Julia ignored my call to thirty-three years ago when I was on the couch watching the U.S Open with baby Julia crawling around at my feet. There was this incredible putt from beyond the green, so I leapt up to follow it in and stepped on baby's hand. I wasn't this big back then, but I've always been a big guy, so you can imagine."

"Come on, you had zero memory of that?"

"Even less than zero. So when was the last time you saw your chin?"

"That's one of those things that's just unknowable."

"Did you have a beard last week?"

"Seriously?" I'm tempted to open my eyes and make the joke that I want a refund.

"Did you have a beard when you started grad school?"

"Yes sir."

"When you met Isabel?"

"She never would have gone out with me if I didn't."

"What about during your first shitty office job?"

"Pulled on it all day long."

"You're disgusting," he shakes his head, pretending to be offended. "What about when you graduated college?"

"The photo on my parents' fridge doesn't lie."

"When you started college?"

"My roommate called me beardy. That was at my second school."

"And the first?"

I guess I look like I'm deep in thought, trying to conjure up an image to replace a still black screen, or otherwise trying to end a standoff with constipation.

"This is your digging spot, let's dig!" Gutwein says. I can feel him grinning with big, twitchy eyes.

Gutwein switches off the lights and clicks the door shut. For such a large and inconsiderate man, he becomes remarkably silent; no sniffling, no sighing, no flipping through papers, no throat clearing, no shifting or swiveling in his chair, no heavy breathing. I drift into the halls of my first semester dorm. Everything is blurry like when you try on your friend's glasses because you think you might look cool in them. Some physical details come into focus. Exposed brick. My roommate's Nickelback poster. My Michael Jordan poster. My roommate's endless stash of processed cheese product and cracker packs in a plastic crate under his bed. Under my bed, a Gatorade bottle I used when not wanting to walk through the common space to the bathroom when certain people were out there. I enter the common room: wood framed, maroon cushioned couches, gray carpet, beetle corpses, floor to ceiling windows looking out onto the quad. Still in the common room my chest becomes heavy and panicked. I want to open my eyes, but Gutwein whispers, "You're right there. Don't let go."

I retreat to my room. Wee hours of morning. I watch myself sleep. A drunken, scratchy voice jostles me awake. It's the kid across the hall, Owen McDermott, a local, a triple legacy, a charmer. He provides our floor with weed and rides to the grocery store and hosts "open office hours" whereby you chill on his bed, he smokes you up and takes notes on any "fundamental life issues" you're having, then helps you come up with an "active solutions plan," which includes drawings and pie charts and Venn diagrams, part fun and silly, part earnest and practical.

I went to his office hours once, hoping to cement our friendship, but after we got nice and high and shared some one-liner jokes, he said, "So, what is it that's eating at you these days?" I insisted, "I really have no problems unless you would count armpit stains on T-shirts." I laughed expecting we'd laugh together, but his eyes became suspicious and confused, as if he was no longer sharing smoky air with a fellow floormate, or I had undermined an activity that so many of our peers found cathartic during the throes of freshman anxiety and mania. I continued to insist. Finally, he said, "You're as stubborn as my grandpa," then he let the THC take him somewhere far away from me. From then on I knew he had exposed something about my core that no one else had uncovered. He looked at me with skepticism and concern and pity and an ounce of fear, but he kept his distance, no longer tried to get me to budge. When I saw him, my chest knotted up and I became short of breath. I'd think about my mom and wondered what my family wasn't telling me. I had short bursts of anger, but after punching the bed or kicking the wall, my chest relaxed, and I'd feel relieved I was the younger child, the one who wasn't burdened with family secrets, and I'd go on with my day, gliding through it.

From the common room his voice gets louder. His audience: one of the girls from our hall, Cathy Heinrich, whom I did a Thursday night ab workout with and whom I once briefly and awkwardly kissed. He does the talking and she does the laughing. He's referring to someone they both know. Not an entirely mocking tone. He's calling him Mr. Happy. Someone who takes himself too seriously, wanting everyone to love him, yet never real, just never acts real with us, doesn't truly want to get to know us, pampered, emotionally repressed, never opens his heart, never tells us anything real, put only his signature on the card for Emily's family. I never catch a name other than Mr. Happy, but who else would it be? When I go out there I'm wearing only boxers. He looks amused and embarrassed, like he was just given a gag gift that crosses the line. She looks afraid, like she has seen a half-naked man do something ugly before. I pin him against the wall, but he's stronger than his baggy clothes let on and after I let go of his throat and land a few solid punches in his middle, he takes control. He wrestles me away from the wall, holds me in a headlock, and says multiple times, "This didn't have to happen," then he releases me and makes a show for Cathy smoothing out his shirt and stretching his arms. They slip into his room and I go over to the coffee table where a row of dirty shot glasses have been left. I plop down on the couch. I pick up a shot glass and smell it—tequila. I'm not a program. Owen McDermott can't simply look me in the eye and determine what I'm thinking and what I'll do next. I'll show him that all that's pushed down inside of me, all that's hidden from me and smoothed over doesn't make me less human. I'll show him that I'm made of flesh and blood and that I could wake the entire dorm, maybe the entire college, in shrieks and screams. I break the shot glass against the table, then take a jagged edge and smash it into my chin.

I open my eyes. Gutwein is looking off to the side. His eyes are red and squinty, his nose stuffy. I check my phone so he can gather himself.

My skin is tingly and itchy like I've come into a heated room after running in the cold. My legs are jelly, my stomach hollow, my brain still.

"I'm not going to ask you what just happened," he clears his throat, "but it was beautiful. Don't fucking tell anyone I said that."

"Don't tell anyone I said thank you or that I'm admitting you've had a very minor positive effect on me. Most importantly, you saved me a ton of money. I promised Isabel I'd go to a hypnotist."

"Lunch is on you tomorrow. Now get the fuck out of here."

It occurs to me that my students may have taken the opportunity to impose the five-minute rule and abscond, but I'm relieved to see they're right where I left them, only they have sunk lower in their chairs, their legs kicked out further into the middle of the circle.

"So?" Shay says.

"You're right. There's something under my chin."

"You thought we were messing with you?" Isto says.

"I didn't want to believe it. But hey, thanks for encouraging me to shave. I'm not joking, it's usually not good to conceal things with thirteen years of body hair."

"My idea," Shay says.

"So was that the point of this class?" Isto says.

"I don't think I'm saying that. I think I'm just thanking you guys. The point of the class, we can leave that up for discussion."

"For when? This is the last day," Isto says.

"I think he means in general," Shay says. "It's something you keep thinking about."

"That's kind of lame," Olivia says. "Teachers are supposed to teach us, you know, like, give us knowledge."

"You guys have been a good class."

"Can we come to your wedding?" Isto says.

"If there's open bar, I'm totally there," Jacob says.

"You should grow a beard," Olivia says.

"Remember," I say, feeling desperate to give some final piece of advice, "writing is all about rewriting in effort to uncover the piece's core. And if your reader doesn't like your work, it doesn't mean it's not a good piece, but it also doesn't mean that it can't be improved. Critique is not something to get defensive about, it's a gift, helps you get closer to the center."

Then, in what feels like one synchronized motion everyone except Stephanie packs up their bags and files out, some offering a *thanks man* or *see ya around* or *have a good holiday*.

"It suits you," Stephanie says, pointing to my chin.

"Thanks," I say, "but meaning what exactly?" It feels pathetic and creepy that I'm seeking approval from my 19-year-old student, but I can't help myself.

"You know, because you're not typical."

I'm pleased that she's replaced the word *weird* with *typical*. *Weird* gets ping-ponged around classroom discussions with temerity, and I encourage students to be more specific, or at least every once in a while reach for a synonym.

"Anyway, I read the essay to my dad, I thought you'd want to know."

"That's courageous of you. How'd it go?"

"First I read it to my mom and she cried and said, please don't read it to your dad, and then she was in a bad mood all day. But then I was sitting there with him and I felt a distance between us even though I was touching his arm, but you know, not like a physical distance. So I asked him if I could read him something I wrote for a class and he said he'd love that. I read it and he got kind of angry, which at first I thought was directed at me, but then I realized it had to do with having to experience his condition from my perspective."

"Sorry he got angry."

"It's ok, I think it was good for him and for all of us. I don't know, it's pretty shitty, excuse my language, but we're also so lucky in so many other ways. It's not like we'd be happy all the time if he was well."

"That's a really mature way of looking at it."

"This class wasn't nearly as boring as I heard it was."

"Thank you," I say. I'm thinking of telling her about my mom or hugging her, but neither of these actions would be appropriate. My silence is keeping her, I'm on the verge of talking, but what more can I say to this young woman? I have no profound ideas or reassuring words. If anything she should be giving me advice. Finally, I say, "I look forward to reading your revision."

She offers a contented nod and smile, and then hurries out as if all of a sudden it occurs to her that she and I are alone.

On the quad I blend into a stream of under-clothed students—many in shorts, open-toed shoes, hoodies in place of coats. Flurries are becoming full flakes. Though the wind whips at and stings my face, I take my time walking the two miles home. I go through different modes of telling the story, tones, ways of portraying myself, ways of portraying Owen McDermott, inflections, even word choice. I feel the gazes of those passing me by—my lips are moving and my arms miming like I'm on an improv stage. I stop at Dunkin' and order eight Munchkins. The lady winks at me and throws in an extra four. I thank her, perhaps too enthusiastically, and she rubs her chin and says in her Eastern European accent, "You look much younger, very cute." And then, "Say hi to her."

I find Isabel asleep on the couch wrapped in multiple shawls and blankets.

"Belly," I say, rubbing her ankle, "I have donuts."

She grunts and mumbles and drools into her pillow. I sit at her feet watching the snow pile up on a fence post. I look at my chin in the reflection of my phone screen, maybe it's not so ugly, maybe I'll stay clean-cut and look my age for a while. The neighbor's dog starts up with his barking. Isabel doesn't budge; she's slept through tornado sirens. I open the box of donuts and hold it under her nose. She yawns and mumbles and stretches herself awake.

"Louie!" she all but shouts. "You're a baby." She takes my cheeks in her hands and smells me. "You're brand new," she whispers, like it's a secret, yet not the worst thing a man can be, her breath wrapping around my face like a warm blanket.

Problems We Can't Name

"I didn't hear Norman this morning," Theo said to Max, clicking into an easier gear. These were the first words since they left the city limits and a formidable headwind forced Theo, the weaker rider, to let Max ride in front. "Didn't even bother to check on him."

"Say what?" Max said, butt lifted off his seat, head slightly turned.

The turning point was in sight, but that didn't mean they were all that close. Out among the bare cornfields they could see across all of Illinois, probably into Missouri, maybe even out to Kansas. It was that flat out there, a fact about Theo's surroundings that didn't bother him. Actually, he liked it. He liked the transparency, nothing hiding around a bend or just over a hill. He liked knowing what he was going to get, what he had signed up for.

Theo wanted to be at Max's side, not a wheel's length behind his muscular haunches, which blocked a good amount of the wind, allowing Theo to keep pace. He leaned forward, dug into his pedals, and swung wide. But the wind slapped him, his quads burned, and he started to gasp for air. Frustrated with himself, he fell back into the drafting position.

They didn't know each other well, but they knew each other better than anyone else in their little central Illinois city. They'd each only been there about a year, Max for a position with a start-up engineering firm, and Theo had a gig living with and caring for Norman Ackerman, a ninety-five-year-old man with no major health problems.

Theo was simply collecting room and board and a modest stipend from Norman's daughter who practiced immigration law in Chicago. Most of the time Norman wanted to be left alone. Every now and then he would invite Theo to sit with him in the living room and give Theo a clue from his crossword or summarize a newspaper article, then ask Theo to give his opinion on the issue. Often Theo wasn't sure how to feel. He could see most issues more than one way, which made him overwhelmed with uncertainty. He preferred not to think about how conflicts in the Middle East could be negotiated or how meat was being produced. It wasn't that he didn't care, he just didn't feel he had the mind to deal with its complexities, which he was okay with. He didn't think everyone with a college degree needed to contribute to solving global problems, or really any problem outside of one's own home.

This time Theo shouted, "How long would it take to ride to Colorado?"

Max glanced back to make sure there were no cars, drifted into the middle of the road and eased up until Theo was at his side. "With this headwind, we'd be all dried up by the time we even got to Kansas." Theo was pleased that Max entertained the question, though slightly disappointed that he didn't come up with an original joke. He'd heard this one before. He may even have invented it himself. They defaulted to aging and fertility jokes. In their earnest moments, they mostly talked about cycling and TV and occasionally told funny stories from childhood, Theo's in Chicago and Max's in Ohio. The next morning Max would be moving to Denver for a more prestigious, higher paying job.

Back in the lead position, Max picked up the pace. He seemed determined to get to the turning point where they wouldn't have to deal with the wind and their ride could become social and enjoyable. He dropped his hands down to the hooked handlebars, reeled his elbows into his sides and lowered his head. His body looked small like a child's, but Theo knew it was solid and full of power. He had playfully punched Max in the shoulder, abs, obliques; they were all the same, hard and firm like an ironing board. Theo admired Max's calves. Though they were swarthy and covered in curly black hair, they reminded him of upside down bowling pins. Theo's calves were skinny and less muscular, more like beer bottles.

When Theo and Max first met, they had both been running. They were across the street from each other going in the same direction. Each used his peripheral vision to keep tabs on the other. For several blocks they gradually increased the pace until eventually they were sprinting. Matching strides, neither man knew when and where the race would end. After a quarter mile or so Theo felt his lunch trying to bring itself back into the world, and so he stopped running. He paced up and down a short stretch of sidewalk with hands on head, elbows splayed out. Max shuffled across the street and slapped Theo on the shoulder. "We'll have to do this again some time," he said, only slightly out of breath. Sweat dripped from the tips of Theo's bangs into his eyes. He squinted and muttered, "God, I hope you're younger than me," then chuckled and offered Max a handshake. Max was thirty-two, three years older than Theo.

Now they made the turn and the wind let up, or rather it now cut across them. Soon they would turn again and the wind would push them along so that if they didn't want to, they wouldn't have to pedal. They had a plan to do a century in the summer. They'd been creating possible routes online and emailing them to each other, with little side comments such as; *at mile forty-three we could stop at the taco truck for lunch*; *not much wind protection in the middle thirty miles*; *worried about traffic*; *should find a few little hills in the state park!* But since Max announced his job offer in Denver, neither of them spoke of the century. They both knew there was not enough time to train, and Theo could tell that even if there was, Max's priorities had shifted.

Max shouted and jerked his bike into the middle of the road. Theo couldn't react in time and rode through the shards of glass from a shattered beer bottle. Max dropped back to Theo's side. They were now within a football field of their turn, an unnamed road marked by a knee-high charcoal boulder with the words *private keep away* etched into it.

"Sorry for the late warning there," Max said. "Was distracted by something my uncle said to me."

"It snuck up on you. Easy not to pay attention out here," Theo said, with great warmth, like a kindergarten teacher encouraging a stuttering student to read aloud. Theo looked down at his front tire and then at Max's. They both seemed fine.

For the first few months they had ran together five days a week. Then Max's knees and Theo's shins started to hurt. There was too much concrete in town and the parks with woodchip paths were too small to make good mileage, so they switched to biking to preserve themselves. They both wanted families one day, though as men they still had plenty of time. They'd joke that biking would help bring their extreme fertility down to a normal level, or that biking would in fact increase sperm count. Regardless, it was a winning situation for them and they had plenty of time to sort it out. *We are men*, one of them would remind the other, and then they'd smile proudly, their faces flushing red.

They turned again, and though they could barely feel it, now the wind pushed them forward. Theo wondered why he still had a hard time keeping up with Max who was upright and coasting. He wondered if it was psychological. His parents often used the word psychosomatic. He already missed Max and felt guilty about Norman. Perhaps these feelings had now occupied his legs making them tired and weak.

Though Theo didn't have much to say, he wanted to be at Max's side. They never said much, they were more doers than talkers, but Theo wanted to hear Max breathe, he wanted drops of Max's sweat to land on his forearms, their legs to spin at the same cadence, their knees and feet in identical positions. Theo found it peculiar that even with a tailwind and a leisurely pace, he couldn't keep up. Maybe he had the flu. Maybe he had given the flu to Norman. He shook his head, looked down at the pavement, and noticed his front tire flat against the road.

They stood in a ditch between the road and a cornfield. Max did most of the work. Occasionally Theo would hand him a tool, hold the wheel steady, and tell Max he was doing a good job.

"So what'd your uncle say?"

"He offered me the company again," Max said. "Told me it was my last chance, has someone else lined up if I don't take it." With his forearm Max wiped a bead of sweat from his temple and gave Theo half a smile. Managing the office of his family restaurant equipment business in Columbus had left Max antsy and unfulfilled. He was one of the few people in his family with a bachelor's degree and the only one with a master's. His family still gave him a hard time for being "too smart for the family business," but assumed that one day he'd come around.

"Is he disappointed?" Theo said.

"I don't know. I said I'd get back to him."

"You did?"

"The thought of all new people—trying to figure out what they stand for, if you trust them, if you actually like them—makes my stomach feel funny like when I drink a second cup of coffee before breakfast."

"You're still young," Theo said.

Max stopped working to offer a nod and then a shrug.

"And being a guy." Theo said this with so much enthusiasm it sounded like he was defending Max, defending himself.

"I need to start fresh," Theo said, holding the bike while Max aligned the tube into the groove of the rim.

"Then you should. You're not even thirty," Max said, slightly out of breath.

"But I'd prefer not to. I want to feel like someone would be disappointed if I left."

"You need to find a nice lady friend."

Theo knew by society's standards it was a despicable act to leave a dead man in his bed to go for a bike ride, but this was his last ride with Max. Had he stopped to confirm Norman's status as not alive, he would then have had to make a series of phone calls and wait around for someone to take him away, perhaps never to see Max again. Maybe Norman was still alive, in which case Theo hadn't done anything wrong other than be a tad neglectful. The body, the phone calls, the arrangements could all wait a couple of hours. Even if he were alive, tomorrow wouldn't be any different; Norman needed little care and what he did need he refused to let Theo have his hand in.

"Do you want a navigator tomorrow?" Theo said, struggling to hold his bike steady as Max pumped air.

"It's pretty much a straight shot across 70," Max said. "Seriously though, you'll find a new riding partner in no time."

"Then perhaps someone to cook and clean while you settle in."

Theo had been engaged. He and Melissa lived in her three-bedroom townhouse in Chicago's western burbs. He worked mornings filing medical records for a doctor who refused to switch to an electronic system. In the afternoons he hung around the house, inventing new pasta salads, mowing the lawn, dusting dressers and tabletops. He enjoyed physical work much more than intellectual. He liked tasks that he could see to completion. Sometimes while doing these activities he thought about what others were doing: his sister finishing a PhD in Sociology, his best friend months away from becoming a dad, his parents in their eighth year of phasing out their practices and transitioning into retirement. Friends and family always wanted to know what he was planning to do next. But he didn't have a plan. He wondered why everyone assumed he was bored and unfulfilled. He wondered why he didn't feel bored and unfulfilled. He took great pleasure in watching Melissa bite into his famous Turkey Reuben or open her closet to find a week's worth of work clothes washed, ironed and hung up. In bed one night, Melissa suggested Theo find something to do that gave him great pleasure and self-esteem, something that required him to use his brain, a *cerebral challenge*, she called it. She insisted he came from a certain type of family and was born with a certain type of brain and certain resources in a certain society that would relentlessly pressure him to do more than simply take care of others. "You should work on becoming an individual who will leave his own little legacy." She hadn't wanted to enter marriage feeling even an ounce of pity or resentment for her life partner-to-be.

Theo noticed Max's cheeks filling with pink. He offered a little laugh because he had no choice. Max laughed too. A young man making the home of another young man—both intending to find wives—would be preposterous.

Instead of turning off at the gas station and taking the most direct route to Norman's, Theo rode with Max back to his little gray ranch house. Out front on the sidewalk, they straddled their bikes and Theo commented that the U-Haul in the driveway looked big enough to move a family of four.

"I'm just being conservative," Max said, "and you've seen my couch."

"I'm just messing with you," Theo said.

"Sure, sure. My sense of humor's a little off today."

"It's all good, man."

Max kicked his leg over his handlebars and gently laid his bike on the lawn.

"Well," Theo said, extending his hand, "no need to draw this out."

Max received Theo's hand and with his other hand he squeezed Theo's bicep, then reached around and slapped his sweaty back so that they were doing a handshake-one-armed hug.

Theo gave Max a squeeze and then they released their grips, their faces red and sweaty and creased from their helmet straps.

"Norman might be dead," Theo said.

"Dead? Might be?"

"I didn't hear him this morning. Not even a throat clear or creak of his reading chair."

"I know he's old, but chances are he's fine, he's never died before."

"I think he's ready to go. Sometimes I hear him get up in the middle of the night and mutter to himself, praying that he joins his wife."

"Then it won't be all that sad, his passing, when it happens."

"But then I'll have no reason to be here."

"Then you can hang out with me for a while in Denver." Max's eyes shot up into his forehead like he was immediately reconsidering his offer.

Theo's pulse quickened. He imagined a life out there, fixing up an old house for Max, sanding baseboards, painting walls, and installing new shelves. He imagined jumping out of bed in the morning to send Max off to work with a stomach full of eggs and fried potatoes and orange juice. He would research century routes with an emphasis on safety and scenery. He even imagined growing old together; their bike rides getting shorter, their knees needing ibuprofen and days off, their arms and legs shrinking along with their bladders and appetites.

"And if Norman is fine?" Theo said.

"Then you still have a job."

Theo imagined what it would be like if Norman was still alive. Norman would read the paper in the living room while Theo would get paid to mostly stay in his bedroom. He would start jogging again and would try to match strides with and shoot glances at other joggers—perhaps he'd join a running club even though he was wary of formalized groups. He imagined riding out among the cornfields fighting the wind, every few minutes checking his tires, his knees aching, praying for no flats, praying for the turning point, trying with great urgency and patience to stretch his vision beyond the golden pink horizon.

Together they rode to the old man's house, letting the tail wind do most of the work. Theo put his bike down in the yard and told Max to wait outside. Norman wasn't in the living room, but there were signs of his morning routine on the side table, a half empty cup of tea and a newspaper and pencil, though the items could have easily been from yesterday. Peering down the hallway, Theo noticed that Norman's bedroom door was left a few inches open. He could count on one hand the occasions he'd entered Norman's room, it was not a space where he was welcome. He walked lightly through the hallway and tapped on the door. No reply, but Norman's hearing was far from perfect. He knocked harder. Nothing. He nudged the door open expecting to see a body for the first time. He worried it would make him ill. But there was no one in the bedroom.

Norman once told Theo he regretted not dying before his wife. They were in the living room, which smelled of lemon tea and old newspapers. "It wasn't your choice," Theo said, reaching for Norman's teacup. But Norman raised his eyebrows and gave Theo a closed-mouth smirk that suggested maybe there was more to tell. "You don't decide these sorts of things," Theo added. Norman held the rim of the mug against his mouth, occasionally sipping his tea. Theo waited. The conversation was cryptic and unsettling, and Norman had started it so Theo felt he was entitled to some closure. But Theo knew Norman's silence meant that he wasn't wanted in the living room any longer, so Theo began to make his way into the kitchen. "Let's just say," Norman's voice pulled Theo back into the room, "had I known what it'd be like, I'm not so sure I wouldn't have gone with her."

Back in the hallway Theo noticed that the bathroom door was closed. His own grandma had passed away on the toilet. An unfortunate place to find someone. To be found. Theo put his ear to the bathroom door. He heard nothing. He could now go tell Max that it had happened in the bathroom and ask if he should call the police or see if the door was unlocked. First he would count to ten Mississippi. This was no time to be hasty. On six Mississippi he still heard nothing, but on seven Mississippi he heard what sounded like a clearing of a throat and then water going down pipes, and a jiggling of that finicky toilet handle while Norman cursed it. Good, Theo thought, all was well then, all was the same as yesterday, but he now felt a deep emptiness in his stomach, which perhaps was hunger; they had gone for a long ride without any replenishment. It must have been hunger. But it didn't feel like hunger.

He hurried out of the house before Norman finished washing his hands. Max was sitting on the front stoop. He was spinning his helmet on his finger like a basketball, sweat glistened on his head and collected around his neck. He looked liked a restless teenager, a patch of hair on the crown of his head sticking up, his leg tapping.

"Well," Theo said, trying not to sound too eager, "I hope you're ready to make good on your Denver offer."

"I'm so sorry," Max said, getting up to comfort Theo, "but what a run of luck he had. Let us all be so lucky." Max rested his hand on Theo's shoulder and gave it a series of gentle squeezes.

Putting his hand on top of Max's, Theo's stomach danced with adrenaline. "No, no, it's not what you think," he said. He waited and studied Max's face before saying anything more.

Yoav Feinberg's Last Year at Home

Sheila, my mom, woke me at the crack to run me around the tennis court with her cheap drop shots and nasty spins, her way of asserting some control over me. Once she whizzed the match-winning backhand over my ear—at which she immediately gave a fist pump and then an apology—we hurried home because the AT&T guy promised to show up between 8 a.m. and 4 p.m., and it was already between those times.

With one hand on the wheel, Sheila dropped the thermos of ice water onto my lap and accelerated through a yellow light. "You're too pale, honey."

I'd heard this one before, but I wasn't some oppositional punk teenager, and it was Saturday, I was in a good mood, and who wasn't prone to dehydration? So I reared back and chugged.

When the doorbell rang, by no means was I dry. Wrapped up in Uncle Donald's latest travel gift—a towel imprinted with a topless Puerto Rican beauty, her hand covering the only spot I had yet to see on a real woman—I raced down the stairs, dripping shower water from my salad plate-sized earlobes, peppering the wood floor with half-foot-shaped puddles.

Given the things Sheila had said about the AT&T guy, I had to see him. *He stopped to rest midway up the stairs. Sweat fell from his nose, elbows, kneecaps—who knows where else! The space he took up. It's a sad case, Yoav. We oughta report it. But to whom? The government? His family? AT&T?*

The naked Puerto Rican covered my lower half, which was good enough. By the congregation's count I was a boy and always would be, though also according to the congregation I was not a Jew, would never be, which was fine by me. My chest was becoming a hair bib, which I would have found unfortunate because it only reinforced stereotypes, which according to my history teacher, Gary Stein, were problematic for many reasons. But I'd yet to come across a stereotype that didn't seem mostly true, and so even the curly hairs closing in on my nipples seemed inevitable, and plucking would just make them grow back more aggressively and thicker, and there must be a good reason for them anyway. If I felt uncomfortable about anything, it was that I was lean and toned with all the working out we did around here, and of course our diet of fish and nuts and fruits and vegetables and a monthly fried egg, and this man behind our front door was said to be the size of one of those lardos we occasionally marveled at at the zoo or the farmer's market, creeping along in a low-rider motor scooter with a liter of Coke shifting around in the front basket. If I didn't see the AT&T guy now, then I might never see him, and if I didn't ever see him, then I would have to keep imagining, and if I had to keep imagining, I might find myself in some dark places.

The figure who stood in front of me was not the lardo AT&T guy, which was disappointing but not crushing. I had other things to do with my life. I wasn't obsessed with meeting people and assessing their diets and exercise regimens and then trying to help prolong their existence. Some people don't want life to be any longer than it has to be, and what exactly is wrong with that? I'd be out of here in less than a year, anyway. I'd go to school in the Northwest where the mountains and ocean rein in cholesterol levels and insist on a carefree mode of operation. But I liked it here, too. I wasn't one of those irreverent, unteachable, know-it-all teenagers who finds his parent old and out of touch. I wasn't champing at the bit to rush off and have new experiences that would be enlightening and progressive and change my entire outlook and make my upbringing, in retrospect, seem mild and Midwestern and provincial. I had nothing to escape, nothing to run from. Additionally, Sheila was a solid housemate, and I wasn't so naïve to think the next person I lived with would be as good of a match. Regardless, it was important I see this whale-sized man, hear his voice, listen to him breathe, determine if he had offspring.

Donald charged through the doorway, gave me an extra-high, extra-hard high five that left my hand stinging, then shot right by me through the kitchen and plopped down on the living room couch. His khaki shorts showed off a piece of his powerful quads, a loose-fitting black polo concealed his minor paunch and encouraged a few chest hairs to poke out at the collar. Under his arm, he carried a scuffed up leather briefcase with shiny gold clasps. Donald was Sheldon's younger brother but had now easily outlived him with no signs of stopping any time soon. He worked long hours and commuted by bicycle, snuck an occasional cigarette, and every couple of years committed to a new life partner. Sometimes he joked about having made babies in exotic lands.

Not all was lost with Sheldon. He successfully left an impression or two on me before giving in to his cardiac disease. He encouraged me to walk on the balls of my feet and taught me how to be gentle when asking for a favor, how to treat people the way they wanted to be treated. I may be making this up, or pulling it from a movie, but I remember shortly before Sheldon went, he covered our faces in shaving cream, mine and then his, and had me mimic his motion, running a bladeless razor up and down my cheek. He always kept a fine brown mustache.

Sheila appeared, still in one of her many baby blue tennis skirts and white tank tops. "How about a glass of ice water?" She didn't wait for an answer to fill up a tall one. "You look thirsty, Donny. Your face isn't always so yellow."

Donald set down the briefcase then scratched a red spot on his calf, making it bigger and redder. When he started to riffle through a stack of papers, Sheila waved him off and led him upstairs into her office to "a proper surface."

It made sense for Donald, as an attorney, to handle the legal matters after Sheldon backed out of life. But that was years ago, and ever since Sheila left the center and started her own practice, more documents emerged for her to sign. I really didn't care what Sheila and Donald were up to because I had plenty to do. If it weren't for the AT&T guy, I'd be playing homerun derby with Logan, or working out a conclusion to my college application essay, which so far was about how people are treated differently based on details as minor as their hair color, body type, or last name, and how this was a social issue with severe consequences. I wasn't sure yet what the consequences were, but the idea felt weighty enough to impress an admissions committee.

On my toes I sidled up the stairs, breath held because if there was something juicy to catch, well, I might as well catch it. I stopped near the top, once Donald's heavy voice became audible. "It's no skin off my back, and if it will help keep you and Yoav alive and well, it'd be foolish not to."

Then Sheila: "What if you find someone you want to commit to? Officially."

Donald sighed. "This doesn't change that."

"I mean legally."

"At this point I don't see it happening."

I took Sheldon's last name, Feinberg, because I wasn't given a choice. Sheila hadn't taken it, which for a while made her life more complicated, but it was a good decision; Feinberg didn't suit her. Logan's last name was Guirl, and though he was blessed with more than adequate height and a deep-ish voice, he felt no choice but to be the first to lift weights and say things like "that chick is a real cunt."

I couldn't blame Sheila. We paid top dollar for health care, and Donald was now our only family around these parts. I backed down the stairs with a pang in my stomach, knowing this was legal and nothing more, but also that Donald would soon find a new life partner and I would soon be off to college and Sheila would still be here in a an old and drafty three-bedroom, two-story house.

At the front door, I watched a pair of squirrels chase each other up an old oak and then a trim young woman in a gray-and-pink sweatsuit push a heavy-duty stroller with thick treaded tires, and then our slightly heavyset mailman carry hefty stacks of paper, whistling and zigzagging between lawns.

•

Later in the day the doorbell rang again. Sheila went to the door with wet hair, black as mine but not nearly as thick. I hung back because I wanted to see how she would greet a man of such mass into her home. I saw how she looked at those people in public, as if they had wronged her, and she had wronged them.

I was surprised to see a slender man with good posture and no sweat rings.

"Looks like Warren was out here just a couple days ago," the man read from a clipboard. "Looks like he did a complete diagnostic and everything looked normal."

"Actually," Sheila said, moving her eyes up and down his torso as if she was waiting for this skinny guy to spontaneously turn into a beast, "everything still looks normal."

"But you did call half an hour ago to make sure someone was on the way, right?"

"Yes, I did, but hey—does Warren only work weekdays?"

I inched closer to deter this man from losing his patience with Sheila, though his face remained indifferent—he'd get paid regardless.

"So you're not having any problems with your DSL?"

"I think it's more of a weekday problem."

"I see," he said. His open mouth closed into a frown. "Hey, I'm sorry, ma'am, but I just have to ask, have I done something to offend you?"

"Oh no, I'm sorry, of course not. We just weren't expecting you. Let me get you a glass of water."

The man shook his head and held the clipboard out for Sheila to sign. "Yeah. Warren works weekdays," he said.

"Now say that ten times in a row," I joked.

The man raised his eyebrows at me, took one last look at Sheila—she was in fantastic shape—and then disappeared into his van.

Fall turned into winter. The AT&T guy thing was over. Sheila never got to save that particular humongous man's life, though there were plenty more out there. I submitted my college applications—a bunch in the Northwest and, just in case, a few nearby. I was on winter break. It was practically Christmas and something like the seventh night of Hanukkah.

When the doorbell rang, I was in my bed thinking of one of Donald's previous life partners who liked to squeeze my arm and say how I was going to be a real charmer. Sheila yelled up for me to get the door, so I snapped myself out of the fantasy, and bounded down the stairs, nearly slipping somewhere in the middle, but given my amazing reflexes, I caught the banister.

There they were, Donald and his new life partner, Tracy, bobbing up and down, huddling together like penguins. Tracy was not quite what I expected. Though she did have wavy shoulder-length brown hair and, from what I could tell, a symmetrical face, she also had both a roundness and softness to her that I'd never seen on any of Donald's previous life partners. Her eyes were energetic yet content, and if you looked closely, which I did, there were a few lines that shot out of them or into them, depending on how you thought about it.

Donald and Sheila sat at the heads of the table. We ate salmon and salad and green beans and brown rice. Donald's left hand was under the table, I suspected on Tracy's thigh. I bit my lower lip and kept from looking. Tracy ate slowly and seemed to be careful never to have too much food in her mouth. It was tough to say what Tracy was. She could have been a Jew. But more than anything, her olive skin, Roman nose, and thick brown hair made her ethnically ambiguous. Not that it mattered.

"So speaking of tropical islands."

Tracy had just finished telling the story of how her parents met. Back in the early '50s in Jefferson City, her dad had a paper route, and claimed he accidentally hit her mom in the back with a wild toss. No one had spoken a word of tropical islands.

"Tracy and I have decided to get married," Donald said.

Of course Sheila and I were psyched for Donald and adding personnel to our little family, huge! But for some reason we both fell silent. They waited, their faces glowing, their breath held. We waited too. I was waiting for Sheila. She was the adult and should have known what to say. She was waiting for me; I could still get away with making mistakes. Donald and Tracy looked like little kids waiting to be given permission to go play. I just couldn't take it any longer. "Mazel Tov!" I said. That much Hebrew I had learned. What else was there to say?

Their frozen faces grew into grateful smiles.

Sheila stared into the kitchen as if waiting for a pot of water to boil or a timer to go off. She wore the same expression when we were tied six to six in tennis and I told her I didn't have it in me to play the tiebreaker: disappointed yet understanding, intrigued but not wanting to ask why, rejected though convincing herself not to take it personally.

"We're headed to Isla Mujeres to celebrate," Tracy said.

Donald had meandered his way to the little Yucatan island the year he took a leave of absence from college. On his recommendation, it was on Isla Mujeres that Sheila and Sheldon completed their first week of married life. I imagined Donald and Tracy holding hands on a narrow street lined with yellow and blue houses, a younger half-Mayan version of Donald passing by, both men pausing, considering, calculating. I imagined Sheila and Sheldon in aviators and patterned swimsuits lying out on warm sand under a coconut tree, in front of a sea of placid turquoise, thinking *this is nice*, and wondering, *what is to come?*

"Hope you don't run into any old friends," I said smiling. What Donald had done or not done abroad had been a long-lived family joke, but Donald shot me a glare that said *this joke is no longer*.

"My mom says we oughta jump out of an airplane before we become arthritic, but I've never been out of the country and Donny is terrified of heights." I wondered if Tracy's parents lived nearby, if Donald and Tracy would have a wedding, if Tracy was young enough to give birth. I smiled at the possibilities, though I didn't want to get my hopes up. Since my highly anticipated entry into the world, our family had only downsized.

Sheila jumped in with, "It's a magical little island."

Donald slung his arm around Tracy and she slapped a hand onto his thigh. They grinned at each other as if no one else was in the room.

"Though be careful not to get too attached," Sheila said.

•

The next day at school I was feeling all charged up and got into it with Gary Stein. He prompted us to make a list of significant actions taken by Thomas Jefferson and decide whether they were more Jeffersonian or Hamiltonian. I got stuck on this and pushed back during class, which escalated to an exchange of some nasty words and wild gestures between Gary and me, which ended class fifteen minutes early. Gary used the remainder of class to call Sheila while I stood by and listened to him repeatedly use the words "irreverent" and "unteachable." All of this because it didn't make sense to me that anything Tommy did could be anything but Jeffersonian given that he, Jefferson himself, was the one doing the doing. But Sheila wasn't the type to punish or even take sides. "As long as you're respectful, Yoav, you can say practically anything." I guess that was the problem. Stein was a nice enough guy, but like so many men I'd dealt with, he had a chip on his shoulder. I joked with Logan how this whole debacle was so Steinian while playing with my attempted mustache.

Sheila and I only had a few more months together, so you'd think we'd hang out a bunch, make the most of what was left, but in reality we'd been giving each other extra space, trying to get used to the next phase. We were still paying top dollar for health care so I guess the deal between Sheila and Donald never went through. Perhaps Donald met Tracy the next day and with the papers prepared and ready to be signed, a prophetic sense of uncertainty overtook him. Donald and Tracy stopped over every so often, but they were busy with work and wedding planning and Sheila wasn't herself around them, she now struck a tone of host more than family member. I'd been accepted by a couple of schools out West and a couple around here and only had another week to make my decision. When Sheldon made his exit, Sheila and I made a pact. But its intention was to protect *me*. I was a child. Sheila was an adult and had been for a long time. Now that we were both essentially adults, contracts as such expired and everyone won, so it was probably just a courtesy that I was considering schools around here.

Sheila was already in her bike gear, eager to hit the roads since she didn't get a morning workout in. But I was so hungry I felt like I might pass out. I opened all the cabinets and the refrigerator several times, but there was only raisins, bananas, apples, cereal, pretzels and cans of tuna. Nothing appealed, nothing seemed substantial enough. Finally, in the depths of the freezer I found a frozen pizza that must have been years if not a decade old, perhaps pre-Sheldon's departure. Its plastic packaging was covered in frost. I cooked the old pizza for fourteen minutes until it was crisp and steamy and ready to eat, but then I couldn't find the pizza cutter. Hiding the pizza cutter struck me as a funny thing to do, but I didn't take it personally nor did I appreciate the gesture. I could have used a knife, but I decided I wanted to eat the whole pie and wanted to take it down fast so it felt like a greasy anchor weighing me down, and I wanted to feel indigestion and maybe even nausea, so I didn't bother cutting it or even stopping to breathe. Sheila sat with me nodding in unison with each bite, the straps of her helmet bouncing off her cheeks. She must have been amazed the way I could put it away. She must have been disgusted. Halfway through she went to the utensil drawer and with no extra effort pulled out the pizza cutter and brought it to me. I guess I didn't look hard enough. Or sometimes you just don't see the thing you're looking for. Anyway, I let it be and shoved down every last crumb, every last flake of cheese, waiting for my body to instantly change.

Sheila and I rode side by side, but we didn't speak, except for her occasional "car back" or "pothole." A few blocks before home, Sheila started to pick up speed without even the slightest signal that it was go time. So I locked into my pedals, dropped my hands down, and made it burn. I flew by her, and then she lifted herself slightly off the seat, leaned forward and passed me back. She probably thought she blew me away, because midway up what we call "the hill," where your calves seriously start to burn, I saw a white van in someone's driveway with the AT&T logo and pulled off the road.

    I walked around the back of the house. A large man, not the largest I had ever seen, was poking around in a breaker panel. On my toes, I went slowly towards him. He turned towards me. His forehead sweaty, his cheeks red.

"Mr. Smith?" he said.

For Christ's sake, did I actually look like I could belong to a Smith family? "I'm a neighbor," I said. My bike helmet probably concealed my age and some of my more "ethnic" features, though my sloping nose was in no way obscured. "I was hoping to ask you a few questions."

"You'll have to call it in, pal." He sighed and went back to the panel.

By now Sheila was probably over her victory and starting to worry. I had seen what I needed to see, a large man who seemed to have a fair amount of life left, doing his job by the book. I had heard his surprisingly clear voice and soft breathing, so I should have been on my way. But I looked at him again trying to determine his age. He seemed to have none. He could have been as old as Donald or as young as Logan's older brother, and why this mattered I wasn't sure. But I couldn't stop looking at him and not because of his size, because he wasn't nearly as large as Sheila's description, but perhaps because I kept noticing more details, like how he leaned to the right, a scar on his forearm, a patch of gray hair on the crown of his head, a brown freckle on his neck, a white cloth creeping out of his back pocket. It would be nice to see such details on everyone, to think of a person and see in your head the littlest things that made them.

"How about dinner tonight?" These words spilled out of my mouth. Clearly my brain played no part in this. Clearly I needed water and a good stretch. I wasn't sweating, but my cheeks radiated heat, my legs rubbery and weak.

He shook his head and a couple drops of sweat flew through the air. "I've had some funny offers, but this is a first. You'll have to call it in."

I was stunned. Afraid. Paralyzed. Not because he said no, but because I had done something I thought only Sheila was capable of doing. I wanted to tell him it wasn't me talking. I looked around for the speaker: a hopping robin, a neighbor's Boston Terrier, him and me.

"I'll tell you what. Give me fifteen minutes and then I'll give you some quick advice."

I must have looked like a real sad case, or he was just trying to get rid of me.

"Wonderful, thank you, sir," I said.

"You betcha."

Now I was light-headed. The man's figure was becoming blurry. I felt it happening again. I tried to fight it. I clamped my mouth shut and bit my tongue, but the words, though muddled, pushed through. "You should take the rest of the day off and go home. It's pretty dang hot out. Just go home and—"

Now he looked like he could be any man, any human being, any being, his figure dark blue and fuzzy, pixilated, a blob. He moved towards me in slow motion. What must have been his mouth opened and closed. I listened, but there were no sounds. I touched my chest and found my heart. My good old heart was still holding down the fort, but its beat was slow and faint. I tried to reach out and touch him, to grab him, but I was just clawing air. And then my knees buckled, and I dropped to the ground, where until the AT&T guy lowered himself on top of me, pinched my nose shut, and breathed long slow breaths into my mouth, I slept soundly, dreaming of a giant nose I used to know with coarse hair spilling out, merging into a fine brown mustache.

A Home for an Eggplant

There is an eggplant on the countertop. It has us both pissed off. We don't have time to cook this hideous thing, Arpi says now, though yesterday, she called it beautiful. I'll put it on Craigslist, she teases, but I'm never quite sure when she's joking.

These are the days of the Craigslist Killer. Two of his victims were found in hotel rooms on our side of the river. They had already done it this way with dozens of strange men who at worst pulled their hair and called them names. How were they to recognize a man who would bind and gag them and leave them without life?

I make sure the door is locked, then grab the eggplant. Our apartment ceilings are tall. Too tall. If a little one ever arrives, perhaps we'll re-sign our lease and I'll build a second floor—a ridiculous idea. I toss the eggplant into the air to use the extra space, and clap three times before I barely catch it. I haven't accounted for its smoothness.

It's a baby, not a football, Arpi raises her voice then shoots me a thin smile that says she's only half joking.

I consider the idea of Arpi and me trying to conceive an eggplant. With that in mind, making a human baby should be a cinch. We have only been at it for months, but it might as well be years because I have known since the moment I learned about Murphy's Law that I will never be a biological father, that everything I imagine can go wrong, will indeed go wrong. One day, after we sign adoption papers, Arpi will ask me to tell her a secret and I'll let it slip. *Yes, Arpi, I know. It's a big fucking secret. Huge! And I never should have kept it. I never should have thought it in the first place.* Arpi's turn: *You can't stop worrying for seven lousy minutes? So your arches, metabolism, cholesterol, everything I signed up for stops with you? You never should have told me. I always assumed it would be me.*

Ah ha, Arpi shouts from the bedroom.

I wonder if she's reading my mind.

Yeah? I shout back.

No answer.

Arpi, what's going on in there?

Nothing, she says. I just wanted to make sure you're still here.

Tonight we throw out a soft tomato and a handful of wilted spinach, three sweaty corn tortillas and half a dissolving cucumber. The eggplant is one day closer.

It's not the end of the world, Arpi says, standing over the garbage can, an unconvincing shrug.

We don't know that, I say.

I'm not perched on the toilet while Arpi showers. I'm not listening to hot water pound against her back and rinse the suds from her golden skin, offering an occasional deep breath to assure her I'm just on the other side of the curtain and haven't left, I won't ever leave, anyone will have to get through me before they get to her, unless they manage to scale two stories of brick wall and bust through the window above the shower—our favorite window, the one that sometimes perfectly centers the moon, as if it were on a TV or a computer screen—then they'd get to her first. Instead, I've tiptoed into the kitchen and pulled the garbage out from under the sink. It reeks of rotten vegetables and coffee. As usual, I stink like a man, not young, not old, not middle-aged, a farmer's market in a men's locker room. I chuckle at the thought even though it's not a perfect analogy. Arpi loves how I smell. She calls it: *good bad.* Hovering over the lip of the garbage, tallying up the calories of our waste, I reach in and grip the tomato like a changeup, and pull it off a coffee filter. I press gently to feel what life is left. Its skin caves in. The bottom is turning dark purple or brown and its curve has flattened. I see why Arpi deemed it unworthy for salad, but in my palm, feeling its wholeness, what remains of its roundness, I wonder if there is another place for it. I turn on the faucet to free the tomato of coffee grounds and random specks of waste. I'm not sure what I will do next, perhaps simply lay it back in the garbage a little cleaner than before, a little better situated. Or maybe I will hide it in the depths of the fridge, out of sight.

The faucet is still on when Arpi yells from the bathroom. Her words bounce around the living room, muddled and indiscernible by the time they get to me. I turn off the faucet, imagining her soapy head under a cold trickle all for the sake of bathing one sorry tomato. Or perhaps a moth flew into her mouth. They seem to be gone ever since we threw out the infested container of couscous, but they have been gone many times before.

She yells again much, louder. Lawrence! Lawrence, come here already!

For a moment I let myself wonder if, the one time I betray our evening routine, some pervert, our neighbor whose fiancé we've never seen, a stranger, the Craigslist Killer, has noticed a lit-up bathroom and decided to give in to his animal urge. We're all human beings. Tomato still in hand, I bound through the living room and into the bathroom, ready to peel off any size man.

The shower curtain is pulled open, the window sealed tight, the moon occluded by a cloudy sky. Arpi shivers, fists covering nose and mouth, elbows squeezed together just above belly, which as usual sticks out a smidge but not any more than that smidge. Water drips from her chin, fingertips, and knees.

What happened? I say. You okay?

The humid air reeks of Arpi's sweet shampoo.

Just wanted you to hand me a towel.

I put the tomato on the toilet cover then unhook the towel from the door and wrap it over her shoulders.

And? she says, pointing to the toilet.

Oh, just wanted to see if we couldn't salvage it for a grilled cheese.

Shit, they're back! Arpi shouts.

My head is buried in the fridge carefully placing the eggplant, as if it stands a chance. I put it next to the other eggplant, the severed one that's all wrapped up in plastic.

As always, I lower the blinds, not wanting any witnesses, then Arpi offers me the cookbook and points to the little carbohydrate-eating moth camouflaged by the cabinet's wood molding, but I don't take it this time. My hand is flat and firm.

I swat too slowly.

Don't worry about that one, Arpi says. We have to find the source anyway.

I have already scraped dozens off the walls. Arpi wants to evict them more than I do but claims her aversion to killing is greater than mine. I think it has more to do with my aversion to an upset Arpi—the squishing is just an action—but then en route to toilet, body in hand, every so often a flutter of a wing, a flicker of life.

There it is again! Arpi shouts. She follows the moth with her pointer finger.

I pretend not to see it.

In our living room I once trapped a roach with a jar. Arpi said it was too big to kill so I let it free in the parking lot. An occasional centipede clings upside down to our bathroom ceiling. I wonder if it's always the same one. Arpi says they're nocturnal, non-aggressive to humans, and feed on spiders and other little bugs. She reads this off Wikipedia. Not a single rodent, but I occasionally wake to a thud or scratch in the wall. Out back, pairs of raccoons dig through the dumpster, just another stop as they traverse the city. There must be dozens of others. I wonder how closely they pay attention to us. I wonder who was here first and who will stay. Our lease is up in a few months. Mrs. Aaronson is tired of our stalling and one day soon will let strangers into our apartment to marvel at the extra space between the ceilings and the floors and try to visualize their lives in place of ours. We don't want to re-sign prematurely, it could still happen, but we also don't want to move into a bigger place for no reason.

I open the fridge and survey our fruits and vegetables. The arugula is getting close, some of the leaves are starting to curl up. The grapes have two days max. I touch a few of the softer grapes then touch the shallow grooves under my eyes.

The Moosewood cookbook called for two-and-a-half eggplants, but at the store, Arpi, recipe in hand, insisted on a fourth, because a third eggplant would have been severed and left without a companion. I scoot the eggplant and the severed half even closer together.

Arpi's mother calls to announce she might give in and get a cell phone. But really she wants to know if we're okay, if we have news and how she can create a new folder on her desktop. I hear Arpi laugh and cry, and yell at her mother, and tell her she hopes to see her soon.

Arpi invites me into the shower. I'm behind her, hands kneading shoulders when we start to try again.

This could be it, she says.

What? I say, out of breath. Could be what?

The time it works, she says.

I stop.

Or maybe it worked last night, I suggest, hoping denial and positive thinking will inspire the very best odds.

I start up again.

I force a mental image of a split-open pomegranate, clusters of brilliantly red fruit, or are those seeds? Arpi says it's the most potent symbol of fertility.

Go ahead and finish, she says. Whenever you're ready.

We hit our top speed.

Just before I completely let myself go, I notice the shower curtain is the color of eggplant, which may be the same color as dried blood, I can't quite remember. I try to think pomegranate, I try to slow down, I even try blueberries and mangoes, some middle ground, clenching muscles, pulling them inward, as if it's even up to me, breath held, breath pushed out and then, still on eggplant, eyes closed, it ends.

I get home from work and there is the eggplant on the countertop. I laugh because I think it's a joke. An entire sick day and this is what she comes up with?

I find Arpi in the bedroom with her laptop on lap. That might be bad for our chances, I say, pointing at the computer.

My vagina is in my shoulders, Arpi reminds me. Come over here and give me a massage.

I start up lightly.

Your hands feel very loving, she says. You'd never kill me, would you?

Not unless you tell me to. Now what's in it for me? I say. No such thing as a free massage.

You warm my nose, I'll give you a handful of raisins.

Ha, good one! I say, even though I'm unsure of the reference. And the eggplant? I say.

I put it on Craigslist, Arpi says.

She is fond of this joke.

Martha will be over any minute to pick it up, Arpi says.

Martha? I say. Oh, your co-worker.

I saw a movie today about a man who poisoned his wife. You'd never do that, would you? Martha from the Internet, she says.

My hands stop working. This is not a Martha, I think. It's unlikely she's even a woman. Women don't go to strange homes. They can't afford to. Not these days. At best, this Martha is planning a petty joke. I hate to think what it could be at its worst.

What about the Craigslist Killer? I say.

What are the odds? she says.

•

Arpi sends me to the door. She says her stomach is still bothering her and it's a man's job to give vegetables to strangers. The eggplant is still cold from the fridge and seems less soft than the last time I felt it. I leave it on the counter in case I need both hands. Through the peephole I see two figures, each with curly blond hair spilling out of a winter hat.

Who is it? I say.

It's Martha, a woman's voice answers.

I unlock the door and open it slowly. The taller woman has a hand in her jacket. I assume she has a pocketknife or at least some Mace. Neither woman seems surprised that I'm a man. Their puffy jackets and red cheeks make me feel old enough to be their dad.

You do this a lot? I say. My voice is a little higher than usual. I don't want to scare them.

First time, says the shorter woman who happens to look like a Martha.

We figured at the very least it'd make for a good story, says the taller woman.

I get the eggplant and hand it to Martha.

Disclaimer, it's a little past its prime, I say.

She tucks it into her jacket.

So you're not scared of me? I say.

Should we be? Replies the taller one, ready to pull her knife.

The ceiling is dropping, the walls caving in. I've spent too much time in here, waiting, worrying, calculating the odds of life, the odds of death. I step through the doorway and join them in the cold. They step back and make a little extra room for me. I turn towards the moon's glow but through the corner of my eye catch a look they exchange which says, This guy is old, not much older than us, perverted, normal, dangerous, harmless, the kind of guy whose wife posts on Craigslist. And finally the look says, What are we still doing here?

Best not to be, I say.

Huh? You want it back? Martha says.

Before I can tell them it's best not to be terrified, but it's also best to be prepared for the worst, but if you're prepared for the worst then you might be terrified, but if you don't prepare then you might worry that you're not taking care of things, I hear my name, first and last, shouted from too deep inside our apartment to determine the nature of Arpi's tone. I will thank Martha and her sidekick and then retreat, excited and nervous at the possibility of news.

But the young women are no longer in front of me. The eggplant nestled into Martha's chest, they skip through the darkness, joking and laughing, patting shoulders and backs, never turning around. Further down the street, I see a long-limbed figure emerge into a patch of light. The women move towards him and he moves towards the women. Soon they will decide whether or not to make eye contact. But the women stop walking. With breath held, I wait for them to turn around, or cross the street, or pull out a weapon, but they do none of these things. The man gets within one sidewalk square of the women and then stops. There is hand gesturing, shoulder shrugging, head shaking, head nodding, and finally Martha pulls out the eggplant and holds it in front of the man. The man nods and takes it from her, tucking it under his armpit and disappearing down a side street. I wonder if accepting the eggplant was a joke for these women, simply something to do, a dare, a game, a test. Or perhaps they were serious about putting it to good use with big plans to make eggplant parm, but their plans changed, as plans often do. I watch them move further into the night, wanting to yell after them, Thank you.

I go inside and open the refrigerator, pull out the severed eggplant and massage it with my thumbs. It is too hard in some places, too soft in others. I put it on the counter and let it be. Arpi calls for me from the bathroom. Her voice gentle and serious, tells me, *something* has happened.